Broken Tether

To Shirley:
Always appreciate freedom.
Stay untethered.

Linda Clifford

LINDA CLIFFORD

BROKEN TETHER
Linda Clifford

ISBN (Print Edition): 978-1-66781-580-0

ISBN (eBook Edition): 978-1-66781-581-7

© 2021. All rights reserved. No part of this publication may be reproduced, distributed, or transmitted in any form or by any means, including photocopying, recording, or other electronic or mechanical methods, without the prior written permission of the publisher, except in the case of brief quotations embodied in critical reviews and certain other noncommercial uses permitted by copyright law.

Contents

Chapter 1: Fahima—Exile 1

Chapter 2: Fahima—Carcass of a Child 5

Chapter 3: Roya—Circle of Women 9

Chapter 4: Uzra—Heed My Words 16

Chapter 5: Fahima—What to Do? 19

Chapter 6: Roya—Designs of a Mullah 25

Chapter 7: Fahima—Allah Save the Children 28

Chapter 8: Kashar—Why We Fight 32

Chapter 9: Roya—Escaping the School of Malice 36

Chapter 10: Uzra—The Prodigal Daughter Returns 41

Chapter 11: Roya—Ticking Clock 45

Chapter 12: Fahima—Time for Action 49

Chapter 13: Fahima—The Quest Begins 54

Chapter 14: Fahima—Who Will Be Our Male Escort? 57

Chapter 15: Uzra—One Son 60

Chapter 16: Fahima—Life's Tragic Balance 65

Chapter 17: Roya—Village Girls 69

Chapter 18: Fahima—A Prayer to Allah 74

Chapter 19: Uzra—Word is Spreading 76

Part II: The Journey Begins 78

Chapter 20: Hawa—Sacrifices 79

Chapter 21: Fahima—First Night 84

Chapter 22: Roya—Direction? 88

Chapter 23: Roya—My Clever Student 91

Chapter 24: Kashar—Dangerous Liaisons 95

Chapter 25: Fahima—The Agreement 99

Chapter 26: Rahmat—Fahima's Quest 102

Chapter 27: Fahima—Girls Under Siege 107

Chapter 28: Roya—Send in the Women 115

Chapter 29: Fahima—Another Danger Overcome 121

Chapter 30: Kashar—Secrets Unfold 125

Chapter 31: Fahima—Peace in a Mosque 128

Chapter 32: Fahima—Leg One to Bamyan 131

Chapter 33: Omar—Boy Soldiers 136

Chapter 34: Roya—Enemies Abound 142

Chapter 35: Fahima—Drug Lord's Hostage 145

Chapter 36: Kashar—Extraneous Rescue 153

Chapter 37: Fahima—Moving On 156

Chapter 38: Rahmat—Sons to Save 160

Chapter 39: Roya—New Ally 165

Chapter 40: Kashar—Hostage Plan Goes Awry 170

Chapter 41: Noor—Reunion 176

Shafika—Reunion 178

Roya—Reunion 180

Sarah—Reunion 183

FAHIMA—EXILE

Kabul, Afghanistan, 1996

"Fahima, please keep your burqa on, you know it is now required," pleads Rahmat as he carries an armload of clothing to the waiting vehicle.

"Rahmat, I can't see where I'm going in this ridiculous costume of modesty," Fahima huffs in utter frustration. "Besides, it is so hot!"

"I know, darling, but we must comply. The Talib are watching. Let us try to finish gathering our things, load the car, and begin the journey back to Dand. I'm glad you were wise enough to send the children ahead to my mother's. It was risky, but it makes this final move easier." Rahmat finishes putting a cardboard box in the trunk of the vehicle. On top of the assortment of household items are pictures of their two teenagers, Roya and Ghulam.

"Rahmat, what are we going to do in Dand? How will we make a living? The Taliban will no longer allow me to work. What will you do?"

"I assume Kashar will take Ghulam and me for the militia."

"Militia! Please, Rahmat, I don't want a teenage boy involved with the violence. Kashar and his thugs are as bad as the Taliban."

"Maybe Fahima, but it will be unavoidable. You are considered a coward if you will not defend your community."

"I understand the need to make a stand for what we believe and to preserve the way of life we want, but the violence is so destructive for both sides. And from an economic point of view, it is absolutely ridiculous."

"I know, Fahima. All these years you have been working with the government to build our nation's economy and now in a matter of months the Taliban has torn it apart."

"It's even more counterproductive to make the females stop working. How can you have a robust economy when half your population is not contributing?"

Rahmat nods and shrugs, then returns to the apartment for another armload of belongings. When he returns he says, "I think this is all we can fit in the car, Fahima. We will just have to leave the insignificant things," as he puts the last pile in the trunk.

"I know, the insignificant things like all our books," she snorts with a sharp note of sarcasm. "The new leaders don't want my delicate gender reading anything outside of the Qur'an."

"Come on now, Fahima, don't you think it will be better back in the village where we were raised? I'm sure the Taliban doesn't have enough soldiers to put a heavy watch on every little village."

"Maybe not, Rahmat, but having to give up Kabul, my friends, and essentially civilization is not a reassuring thought. Our whole way of life is changing. We are going back to our beginnings and waving goodbye to the life you and I have made. Education. Careers. Progress."

The heat and humidity of the Afghanistan summer only accelerates Fahima's dread of leaving Kabul and magnifies the discomfort of wearing the burqa.

"I understand that this is a huge step backward, but at least you will have your best friend, Jahan, in the village with you." Rahmat tries to reassure and soothe her. He then closes the trunk and slides into the driver's seat. "We had better get going while it is still cool."

"You are right, left-brain engineer that you are. My voice of commonsense. Jahan and I can commiserate about the wonderful lives we left because of the Taliban."

"That's the spirit," smiles Rahmat as he pulls the car away from the apartment.

Rahmat moves to turn the radio on and Fahima stops him. "Please, Rahmat, this move is hard enough. Let's not listen to the government's propaganda. I know I must be a chaste woman and obey the will of my husband and every other man who wants to control my life."

"Fati, since when have I ever had control of your life. Hmm?"

"I know, but having to go back home when our lives are bright and hopeful here is distressing. What am I going to do in that dusty little town?"

"You are going to raise your children, wear your burqa, and do what Fahima always does: stay focused and loving."

"In other words, do what is dictated to me, not what my heart and brain want me to do."

"Precisely. Come on, Fahima, these are dire times, but it won't always be this way. This is Afghanistan. Ruling parties come and go here. They have for many generations. At least we are not living in tents and riding camels. Have you ever had to milk a goat?"

"Very funny, Rahmat. Our country should be progressing like others around us, but these religious zealots have pushed us back into the dark ages. How can a third-world country like ours progress when half the population is not allowed to contribute? Women need to participate, to bring more to the culture than babies."

"Admit it, Fati, you are good at making babies. Ours are beautiful."

"Yes, but if given the chance I could do so much more."

"Well, my love, you will figure it out. I would expect nothing less than you running the village with grace and efficiency in your beautiful blue burqa." He turns from the wheel to flash a huge grin. Fahima slides the hood of her burqa back and leans over to kiss his shoulder.

"I love you, Rahmat. Thank you for understanding who I really am." She straightens herself and looks forward through the windshield. She does not turn to look back to see what she is leaving behind. Rahmat puts his hand on top of hers reassuringly and then heads south to Dand.

Chapter 2:
FAHIMA—CARCASS OF A CHILD

Dand, Afghanistan, 2001

Fahima awoke to the distant grind of a truck changing gears. There was a rattle and choke to the engine. As it drew nearer, her head began to clear, the anguished, unsettled sleep that she has been fighting for years dissipates, and the realities of her day seep into her wakefulness.

Within seconds the growling struggles of an ancient vehicle are all that she can hear and then the sounds quell for a moment and a muted thud breaks the morning air at her doorstep. The truck then speeds off.

Now fully aware something has been planted at her door but confused as to what it could be at this hour, she gathers herself and cautiously walks to the door to determine what the first challenge of the day might be. She stands at the door and listens for signs of danger. Nothing. Slowly she cracks the weathered, sundried door and, through the crack sees a small brown foot. Her stomach retches at the sight and her mouth fills with the salty brine of fear and dread. As she widens the door opening she sees the ragged mound of the remains of a child.

A girl. Bloodied, dirty, limp and lifeless. The curious joy and childish energy completely drained from her fragile little form. It was Zahida, a twelve year old from the village, who was sold to a militia man by her mother to feed her younger brothers and sisters. She was dead. Violated and tortured. Fahima looks down and thinks about how the tender sweetness that Allah blesses children with has been wiped away. Gone is the innocent, endearing smell of play and mimic and her wonder at the world. Gone is the hope of love and peace and happiness that children should be allowed to seek in a world that will soon enough throw sorrow and pain and violence upon them. At her doorstop is the carcass of a child.

Fahima kneels and scoops the cold body to her, holding back a scream muted by the total clutch of grief that grabbed her heart and voice. *So cold. Little Zahida's growing bones are growing no more. Her learning heart is beating no more. Her smile nevermore to tell the world that she is a daughter of Allah.*

Fahima looks up to see only the trail of dust left by the truck that delivered this poor daughter to her door. She knew immediately why they dumped Zahida on her doorstep instead of her mother's. She had tried to talk her mother out of selling her. It was happening a lot in the village, since most of the men were gone, poverty and the inability of the women to provide for their families was growing. Fahima had pleaded with her. Offered to share all that she had with her, but the ready money and crying mouths of Zahida's three siblings convinced the struggling mother to take the cash and give up her oldest daughter to a brief life of sexual abuse and violence. *Throw away the females. Defenseless human dolls that undisciplined, unprincipled barbaric men purchase, control, and discard. Females have no value. Women and girls not yet women are nothing but objects to these men. These men are not held accountable for the acts they perpetrate against Allah's women. What cowards! What unholy, disobedient men of Allah's grace and love. They are a plague on our violence-riddled country.* Fahima's thoughts swirl inky and dark as she realizes the evil-coated state of her village and the culture around her.

As the sun continues to rise and the warmth of a new day begins to stir life, Fahima takes the child off the street and into her home, instinctively cleaning her face and hands. She closes her staring, blank eyes, and sits on the rug beside the lost life crying uncontrollably. Her body quakes with the gasps of air she needs to counteract the huge sobs. Her head bobs, almost too heavy to control. Her body is seized with despair and spasms of total weakness. The black plumes of death and grief fill her house, and the noise of her anguish awakens her daughter, Roya.

"Mother, what has happened?" Roya says as the twenty-six year old kneels next to Fahima on the worn rug.

"This is little Zahida. One of your students. Only days ago one of Kashar's men bought her from her mother. Now he has returned her to us in a bundle of violated rags."

"But why did they leave her here?"

"Because they saw me plead with her mother not to sell her. It is a sign they know I am working against them. They want to show me and all of the other women that they are the powerful ones."

"This is very dangerous, Mother," Roya's expression tightens with fear. "It is difficult enough these days without the militia men having specific issues with one of us. Are you frightened?"

"Roya, I am tired of being frightened. I am crippled by the pain that the loss of our children and people inflicts. My own life seems so worthless when I cannot help combat the pain and violence."

"Mother, you can't mean that."

"My strength is being sucked away each time a precious one is sent to Allah and I am left to watch the rest. I am a mother, wife, and daughter. Allah sent me to nurture and care for all around me. Soon my job will be over because no one will be left. The ruthlessness of our own people will sacrifice us all for their ridiculous conflicts and fights."

"Mother, we must not give up."

"Darling, you are so young and so wonderfully idealistic. If you only knew how much I fear for your future. I did not want to give you a world of worry, a world where peace is not allowed. A world where you will awake every morning fearful of what the day will bring. No, that is not what mothers wish for when they bring children to life. I have failed you. I cannot control or change this way of life. I cannot give you a good world to live in and raise your family. Allah has turned his back on the people of Afghanistan. We are souls crying in the wilderness for change, but he does not hear. We have disobeyed and are being punished by our own acts."

"Mother, these acts are not yours or mine. We have not inflicted pain and suffering on others. We have not committed unspeakable acts of violence against others. These are not our acts. Allah will see that and answer our prayers."

"I hope I live long enough to see that that is true. Let's say our prayers and then we must prepare little Zahida to return to Allah. We must gather the other village women and tell her mother."

Fahima and Roya unroll their prayer rugs and tearfully begin their daily prayer ritual.

Chapter 3:
ROYA—CIRCLE OF WOMEN

The mournful, piercing sound of wailing women is beginning to quiet in our dusty, ancient village as the sun sets and evening prayers finish. One by one, women gather in the small house Mother and I share with my paternal grandmother, Uzra. Since my father and brother, Ghulam, were forced to join the militia, the three of us have moved in together to survive.

I returned to this village after some years away. I was forced home from my journalism job in Kabul when the Taliban took power. Now we survive on the small salary I am paid to teach the children of the village.

Today's sad event, the burial of one of our young girls, has sent another current of grief through the entire community of some fifty families. These days, most of those left are women, children, and a few old men. Like many villages, the young boys have been kidnapped or convinced to go with the mullahs to the madrassa, the radical Muslim schools for young boys.

Our adult males have either been killed by the fighting or dragged off to be part of the militias. We have not heard from my father and brother for months. Our days are weighted down with the gray fog of grief and uncertainty. Mother, Grandmother, and I try to stay hopeful that Father and Brother will return, but we know the odds of that are not in our favor. Grandmother Uzra prays to Allah twice a day that they will return before she dies.

Aunt Sakina and her daughters are here. Aunt Sakina is married to Uncle Mahmoud and has two daughters, my cousins Nooria and Shafika with her. Aunt Sakina is younger than mother. I remember when she married Uncle Mahmoud. She was such a beautiful bride. Her skin is light, and then her face was perfectly round with a lovely mouth and expressive dark eyebrows set close over her deep dark eyes. Now she is gaunt. Her eyes have lost hope and reflect the sadness all around.

Shafika looks most like her at twelve years old. Nooria is fifteen, and her face is more oval like Uncle Mahmoud's. Nooria always seems to have a sad, serious look on her face like Grandmother Uzra. The years of not knowing where husband and father are has drained the loveliness from all their faces. Mother silently hugs Aunt Sakina and each niece.

Mother and Grandmother prepare tea while I set out almonds and tangerines. Hosting is very simple these days because we have so little. I so miss the elegant little toffees in their gold wrappers that we always had on the table for guests. The sweetness of our lives has been sucked away by all the poverty the fighting has brought.

Aunt Sakina moves to the courtyard as the girls follow and finds a seat under the old tree in the middle. Jahan, mother's best friend, comes in and she and mother hug each other, then Jahan greets Grandmother with an embrace. Jahan's perfectly arranged hair sets her apart from others in the village. Mother says Jahan has a sense of herself that beams through everything she does.

Jahan is an artist. She generally wears brightly colored scarves that set off the white streak of hair over her left eye, making her jet-black hair even more glamorous. Jahan's illness has turned her skin gray and dull, but the brilliance of her hair reminds us that Jahan and all her creative energies are there under the surface.

Jahan is battling a cancer that has no remedy out here away from the medical care in a big city. She and Mother have been friends since childhood and were the only two girls to leave the village and go to Kabul for advanced education. Mother studied economics while Jahan studied art.

"My friend," says Mother, embracing Jahan and checking her over to see how much more ground she has lost from her illness. Jahan responds by tightly clutching Mother then stepping back and wiping the tears from her eyes. Mother does the same.

"Ah, Fahima, what are we to do? We are losing our next generation too quickly to replace them. You and I are too old and worn out to pick up the yoke and carry the village forward. I am by Allah's grace only here for a short time more." Jahan looks deeply into mother's face for acknowledgement.

"Jahan, it is too terrible to endure most days. Why are we here? Why is Allah allowing this to happen?" Mother says.

"Hello Jahan. How are you feeling? You look lovely today," I say, hoping to distract both from their sad dialogue and brighten the gloom.

"Ah, Roya," says Jahan. She touches my face and says, smiling, "You are such a joy for your mother."

"Aunt Sakina and Nooria and Shafika are in the courtyard. It's cool out there right now. They would love to see you."

"Yes, darling, I would love to see them. See how the girls are maturing," Jahan replies, and then moves through the door to the courtyard.

"She is not looking well," whispers Grandmother Uzra. "Fahima, how long ago was Jahan diagnosed with her cancer?"

"Mother Uzra, I think it has been three years now," Mother painfully responds. "Considering she has had no treatment; I think this is the best we can hope for."

"Such a lovely woman, Fahima. You have been blessed to have her as a friend all these years," Grandmother Uzra watches Jahan greet Aunt Sakina through the open door.

"I know. She has enriched my life in hundreds of ways over our friendship," Mother starts to say something else, but stops suddenly. I think the thought of Jahan not being here is too much for her to think about right now.

"Mother, here is Maky and her little ones," I say as I move to the door to help Maky with the toddler in her arms. Maky is a young mother and distant cousin. She is carrying little Jalil, who is eight months old, while Noor, a mischievous eight year old trails in behind his mother. Maky is married to Ahmad. She is fortunate that Ahmad is away working in Qandahar and has avoided being usurped into the militia. Noor is still too young for the madrassa, but soon the mullahs will be back to get him.

Mother takes Jalil from Maky's arms and bounces him as he giggles and drools down the front of his shirt, showing a shiny tooth starting to emerge through his bottom gum. I say hello to Noor, who is one of my students. He politely greets me and then darts off to the courtyard to see if there are any other boys to play with and to get out of reach of all these ladies.

"Maky, how is Ahmad?" Mother asks.

"I have not heard from him for two weeks, but I assume he is safe. This is such a sad day for Zahida's mother, Alia. I am fearful for my boys being taken by the mullahs to the madrassa, but the fate of girls seems so much more terrible." Maky takes Jalil back from mother and heads to the courtyard to find Noor.

"I am afraid the fate of our boys is no better than our girls," says Grandmother. "Allah is punishing us all."

"Come, Grandmother, there are more coming. We need to prepare more tea," I steady her elbow and we return to the kitchen to heat more water.

Village women continue to fill the house and courtyard. They speak softly and quietly to each other, afraid the very act of talking about it will bring the wrath of the militia down upon them. After about thirty minutes, Alia, Zahida's mother, enters the house. Everyone is silent and looking at her. Mother moves to her side and welcomes her in.

"Alia, we are so sorry for your loss," Mother consoles her.

"Fahima, I know you and the other women of this village think me a monster for selling my Zahida to save my other children, but what else was I to do? I know you would have found another way, but I am not educated like you. I could figure no other way to feed my family. I thought she would be safer and better cared for with him. What a fool I was."

Alia begins to cry and sob uncontrollably. Mother embraces her and tries to reassure her it was the only thing she could have done.

"I should have listened to you, Fahima. My Zahida would still be alive," Alia blurts out. "I have always believed that we women are powerless. That I am powerless, especially without my husband, father, and brothers. You are smart and strong. I am not."

Jahan emerges from the courtyard and joins Mother in trying to comfort Alia. "We are all powerless in this as women in this village," Jahan sputters. "That's how they want us."

Grandmother Uzra steps up. "Come, Alia, let's join the other women in the courtyard. They are anxious to see you and express their sympathies. No one blames you for making impossible decisions to save your family."

Alia bows her head and allows Grandmother to lead her by her sunken shoulders to the courtyard where the rest of the village women are gathered. The children are running and playing around the old almond tree and the bare shrubs dotting the edges of the shaded courtyard. Their laughter brightens the gloom that is overwhelming the group.

Aunt Sakina and Maky approach Alia to hug her and express their sympathy. The other gathered women follow suit, one by one embracing Alia and expressing their regrets while in the back of their minds thinking it could be them or one of their children next.

"All this is your fault, Fahima," says a reproachful young woman at the back of the courtyard. "Your history with Kashar makes our village and our children targets."

"Farriah, you can't mean that," I shout in defense of Mother. I know Farriah as an aggressive, angry young woman. Her younger brothers were taken by the mullahs and her older brother was killed fighting with Kashar's militia group.

Farriah pushes her way through the throng of mourners to the front where Fahima and Alia are standing. "You bring his attention here. You put us all at risk because he is angry with you."

"That's ridiculous," I retort. "You have no idea what you are talking about."

"My mother has told me that Kashar and your mother have been at odds since they were young. Our village is like a constant thorn in his side. He punishes all of us because he hates your mother."

"Farriah, how can you say such things," Aunt Sakina interjects.

"That is malicious gossip, Farriah," I sputter indignantly.

"Please, please, girls," interrupts Mother. "There is truth to what Farriah says. Kashar resents me, and that fact continues to gnaw at him despite the many years that have passed."

"See, Roya," Farriah triumphantly hisses.

"Our village is no different than any other village," Jahan interjects. "The militias come through and take what they want under the guise they are protecting us. Who is protecting us from them? Let's face it, as women we have little value to men beyond our own families. Our culture believes we are less than men. They say the Qur'an teaches this. As women, we are objects to be worked, traded, and used. Even our holy men have no regard for us."

"Zahida's brutal death should be a sign to us," Grandmother Uzra speaks softly and solemnly. "It is time to protect our children, even if our men are not here to help us. The children are the most precious treasure this village can produce."

"Mother Uzra, you are right," Fahima says. "We must act to protect these treasures. Surely that is Allah's will, and He will show us how."

Murmurs go through the courtyard. Just talking this way frightens some. The fear of reprisal for speaking and acting out could bring terrible consequences to the group and the village overall.

Chapter 4:
UZRA—HEED MY WORDS

The village women have left and Fahima and Roya are cleaning up. As I look at my daughter-in-law and granddaughter, I am struck by the vision of a rugged and dangerous road ahead for both of them. My village of three generations is crumbling around us. The future for my family is bleak. My sons and grandson are missing. My granddaughter Roya, who had a bright future with an education and an important job in Kabul, is here in this primitive village wasting her talent and her youth. Nooria and Shafika, my young granddaughters, have no opportunity for education and a better life.

My daughter-in-law is destitute and grief stricken by the state of everything around her. My life is close to finished. I will be leaving this earth in worse shape than I found it. I have failed my Allah and my family.

"Roya, please help your mother by finishing up the teacups and plates."

"Of course, Grandmother."

"Fahima, come sit with me in the courtyard. I am weary after all that has taken place today."

"Yes, of course, Mother Uzra."

We sit in the shade of the almond tree as the sunset paints the horizon in orange and purples. The enormity of the day silences us for a long time. I look at Fahima's hands, quietly folded in her lap. They are cracked and red from work. She went to school to be able to use her mind and have a better life. Now she is here clinging to an existence that is primitive and violent. She is desperately trying to protect her daughter and waiting anxiously for word of her husband and son and their safety.

My old hands are gnarled and worn from the years of life that have passed between them. My fingers are now crooked and painful. These hands have tried to build a better life for my family. Now they are useless to help them get to a better place. They ache all the time, but the ache in my heart is the real pain.

We both sit for a long while without speaking. Finally, I break the silence. "Fahima, you and Roya must leave here."

"No, Mother Uzra, not without you. Not without knowing where Rahmat and Ghulam are or if they are still alive. I must be here when they return."

"Fahima, if you stay here you may meet the same fate they have. You and Roya must go where it is safe."

"And where is safe? There is nowhere in Afghanistan or Pakistan where we can go and be the women we want to be."

"There may be no place where you two can be the women you want to be, but there are places where it is better to be a woman than here. In my years I have seen hope that women will be allowed to learn to read, be educated, and make equal decisions in the family. That progress has been thrown away by the radicals. The women of our country have been tossed back generations to a time when we mean nothing more than goats—bred, worked, beaten, traded, slaughtered. You and Roya must find a better place. You both have educations. You will survive somewhere new."

"I, too, have felt the progress and now the utter devastation of those hopes. And I fear for our Roya and Ghulam and their futures. But leaving here? I do not know enough of the world to imagine where we could go or how we would get there."

"Fahima, you know more of the world than me. But I know and have seen the future by way of the past and things are not going to get better anytime soon. Allah is punishing us for the violent ways we treat our own people. Our men fight amongst themselves. They hate one another and any outsiders. This is not Allah's way."

"I don't know how we got to this state. In my day, things were progressing well with King Zahir and then the Russians. Then the Taliban ran out the good people and replaced our wise and loving leaders with clerics and seemingly sacred religious leaders who have thrown our culture back to the days of Sharia law and Bedouin caravan ways. We were a developing country and culture, now we are back in the dark ages again."

"You and Roya must go. The winds of change are not approaching. Things will get worse before they get better. There is no one or thing to reverse this."

"Mother Uzra, the thought of leaving is just too hard."

"Fahima, you must be strong both for you and Roya. You both must escape this."

"It seems selfish, Mother. How can Roya and I leave and leave you and the rest of the village to fight on without us?"

"You must, Fahima. I beg you. For me. For Roya's children to be."

Fahima grabs my hands between hers and we look into each other's eyes. *I see the understanding and fear in her eyes. I hope she sees and understands the urgency and truth in mine.*

Chapter 5:
FAHIMA—WHAT TO DO?

It has been a week since the tragic death of Zahida. Mother Uzra's words circle in my brain. She is right, Roya and I must leave. Still, I cannot find the courage to take Roya and flee and leave the village women and children behind. These are people I have known all my life. In many ways, their fate is worse than mine and Roya's, but I am not a leader. I am not a rebel. Farriah is correct that I do bring undue attention and aggression to this village because of my past with Kashar. I am responsible—that I know.

How should I proceed? What should I do? Who do I enlist to help us? I must seek some thoughts from others. But who? I hate to burden poor Jahan. She and Rahmat have always been my best sounding boards. Together we have faced our challenges with mutual support and wisdom. We have always shared a listening ear and supportive shoulder. Dragging her into a mission like leaving the village could be more than her diseased body and mind could take. It could certainly hasten her end. Who do I turn to? Will Allah show me the way?

I must stay busy and keep my mind and hands occupied. I'll go to the well for water. A walk in the sun will brighten my thoughts. Seeing other village women and having a pleasant, normal conversation will give me a better perspective. I always love to see the children, although these days they look thin and unhappy as they wait for their papas to return. I know how they feel. We are all waiting. We are all fearful.

The village well used to be such a fun place to go—always news and gossip about the village and those in it. These days it represents being in public and exposed for too long. Everyone quickly draws water and returns to the shelter of their home. The simplest pleasures have been taken from us. Anyhow, maybe I will run into someone interested in visiting for a moment. Maybe encounter someone willing to take a chance on being seen in public talking to the evil Fahima. Ha.

I find the water jug and make my way. It is a hot, sunny day. The dust is thick and the sunlight beaming through it looks like dry rain. As I approach the well, I see a large, brown mutt of a dog trying to reach the top for a drink. He is tall enough stretched on the ledge to see down into the well, but not tall enough to bend his neck and grab a drink. As I get closer, he turns to look at me and begins wagging his tail uncontrollably. I reach the well and give him a good pat on the head, then look around to find something to give him a drink. Seeing nothing, I cup both hands and hold it to his mouth as he happily laps up the warm surface water with his soft pink tongue.

"Pooch," comes a call from behind me, and the dog stops and jumps down. I turn and see Hawa, a friend and farmer's wife, working her way to the well to retrieve the dog.

"Ah, Hawa, is this one of your family?" I inquire with a smile.

"Greetings, Fahima. Yes, this is Pooch. This rascal loves to run to town and get into mischief. He is the master of escape." She lets out a big belly laugh as she ties a small rope around the dog, who is eager to obey and follow her.

"How are things on the farm, Hawa? How are your husband and sons?"

"We are managing. Walizada, our local drug lord, is watching us like a hawk until the poppies are harvested. That is a crop I do not enjoy growing, but because we are doing it for their profit my sons get to stay on the farm."

"And your Omar, how is he doing on his one leg?"

"He is moving well on crutches. Since he stepped on the landmine in the fields, the militia has been generous and let my boys stay to work the fields because their father cannot thanks to them. It is a strange blessing from Allah."

"Indeed. To have your husband and sons around you is truly a blessing."

"Fahima, any word on your Ghulam and Rahmat?"

"Nothing, Hawa. I am always hopeful but understand the reality of our situation."

"How is town life? I heard one of the village girls was sold and then returned as a bloody corpse."

"We buried Zahida, Alia's oldest daughter, a week ago. Hawa, I am desperate to understand how we got to this state. I am totally without hope. I am sick to death of the violence. I am outraged at the state of the village and our country, and the sick and evil world others have to raise their children in. You and I are lucky our children are raised and knew this as a better place than it is now."

"Yes, Fahima, you have said it exactly as it is. Allah is looking down, angry. We are not living according to his wishes. I would say this is not really living."

"Have your sons found wives yet?"

"No, my sons do not wish to bring children into this world, either." Then she lets out a hearty laugh and says, "Besides I work them too hard to think of women and their future."

"Hawa, you are a good mother." I bend down to pat Pooch on the head and give him a good scratch behind his ears, "Even to this four-legged son."

"Being raised and living on the farm I have a different perspective on mothering. I see more four-legged mothers than two," another belly laugh, and Hawa turns to leave with Pooch in tow.

"Hawa, wait a minute. Do you have time to talk?"

"I am waiting for my little Omar to return, so yes. Maybe a cup of tea?"

"Come to my house. We will have tea and chat."

I fill my water jug and Hawa, Pooch, and I walk up the worn path to my house.

"Please come in. You know my daughter, Roya, and my mother-in-law, Uzra, right?"

"It has been some time since I have seen Roya. She is quite the young woman now."

"Hawa, no designs on my daughter just now for one of your handsome sons. Although I do confess, it would be splendid to have grandchildren, no? We have some work to do before this is a proper place for our grandchildren."

"Okay, you are right. Oh, hello Mother Uzra," Hawa adds as she acknowledges my mother-in-law entering our little kitchen. "It is so good to see you again."

"Hawa, nice to see you in town," says Mother Uzra, "Tell me, do you allow dogs in your house?" as Mother Uzra notices Pooch tailing behind Hawa.

"They are my sons, too," chuckles Hawa in answer.

"Ah, you farm people are so generous," Mother Uzra notes with a smile. "Since he is your son he can join us." As she looks down at Pooch at the end of his rope, she rubs his furry back with her aged hands.

"No tea for him, though," Hawa smirks.

I pour tea for Hawa and me and ask Roya and Mother Uzra to excuse us so we may speak in private.

"Hawa," I begin, "Mother believes Roya and I need to leave the village. In my heart I know this too but cannot seem to tear myself away as I continue to wait for the return of Rahmat and Ghulam. As we have already discussed, our village has become too violent and unsettled to raise children. There will be more Zahidas and more and more of the boys taken to the madrassas. We must go and take the children. What are your thoughts?"

Hawa settles her heavy frame on a floor cushion and pulls Pooch next to her and begins stroking his flank. She thinks for a long minute and then says, "I am a simple country woman with my men around me to run the farm. I cannot imagine the lives you and the other village women live, enduring fear and potential violence every day. My husband lost a leg as an adult. I cannot imagine worrying every day that one of my small children will meet the same fate or worse just playing in the village. This is not right."

"So, you understand how we live."

"Not really. But the little I see and know I do not like. I especially do not like the way women and girls are treated. It is true that I am isolated from that because I am out in the country and have my husband and sons who do respect and honor me, but you village women are now their chattel—nothing more."

"Hawa, you are a remarkably bright and strong female. What do you think we should do?"

"Fahima, I believe Allah wants the women of Afghanistan to save their children and themselves from this way of life. You are educated. You are the one to lead them to a better place."

"Hawa, do you believe there is a better place, and do you believe we can get there?"

"Fahima, I believe that if there is not a better place, we women can build one."

"That is quite a statement. Would you help?"

"Fahima, living on the farm I have learned to do many things that traditionally our women are not allowed to learn or do. Necessity teaches us all, with a little help from Allah," she adds with a wry grin.

"You are too much. I wish I were as strong and positive-minded as you are," I reply. "Are you saying you would go with us?"

"I'm not sure. If my husband and sons are allowed to stay and work the farm, I would be willing to help get the children and innocent women of this village to a safer place. I deal with the militia men almost every day. The only reason they don't mistreat me is I have something they want and need, and it is not twelve-year-old girls."

"You and Pooch here have given me hope. Right now, that is a priceless commodity." She and I stand and I embrace her bulky body and feel her give me a reassuring squeeze.

"I hear my little Omar calling for me. Pooch and I need to go," she says as she bends down for Pooch's rope. "Let me know what you need of me. Remember Fahima, Allah is with the weak."

"Hawa, Allah has special plans for you." With a wink I add "and so do I."

Chapter 6:
ROYA—DESIGNS OF A MULLAH

"Students, please remember to take your homework with you if you have not finished your assignments and finish them before prayers this evening. I will review them tomorrow morning." The gaggle of students spring from their chairs and race to the door, the littler boys darting under the older girls, the little girls shadowing the big girls.

It is so strange to see a classroom 2/3 girls and only 1/3 boys and all the older students girls. I guess our girls are lucky they are allowed to go to school. In many parts of Afghanistan, girls are not allowed to attend school.

It has been a long, tiring day. Finding enough materials to adequately instruct all these children is draining. Roya crosses the small, earth-covered schoolroom floor and straightens the chairs and ancient, splintered wooden desks, as she moves to the door to leave. Before she reaches the doorway, a small, dark man enters.

"Mullah Aman, how nice to see you. Allah be with you." *I know why he is here. He never bothers with the school unless he is looking for more boys to send to the madrassa. I must try to hide the concern in my voice.* Mullah Aman is the main religious leader of the village, our Imam, and the man responsible for recruiting young boys to the madrassa. *Thank goodness he has arrived after the children have left for the day so he cannot see how many small boys I have in my classroom.*

"To what do I owe this visit?" I say, as brightly and unconcerned as possible. I do not want him to think I am afraid or on edge.

The small man continues through the doorway and surveys the classroom. He walks past me to inspect the materials hanging on the walls. He smiles at the pile of tiny prayer rugs stacked in one corner and turns to address me.

"Mistress Roya, may Allah be with you," he begins.

"And you, Mullah Aman," I reply as expected.

"How many students do you have these days?" he inquires.

"I have thirty-seven," I say, trying to sound matter of fact.

"And how many are boys?"

"I have to think about that since I view them all as students and do not consider gender," I say.

"You are fortunate to be allowed to teach girls, Mistress Roya. I am a more generous Mullah than some."

"You are kind and understanding, Mullah Aman. I do feel honored to be allowed to teach the girls as well as the small boys. Your wisdom is truly well served." *Hope that was humble enough for him. He is correct about the opportunity he allows the girls in our village to be taught with the small boys. I'm sure he thinks what I teach is nothing compared to what the boys learn in the madrassa.*

"So, how many small boys?"

"I believe I have four that are five or six years old and another eight that are seven to ten. Yes, twelve boys and twenty-five girls. That would be my thirty-seven."

"I see," he says as he pulls on his stubby, gray beard and looks deep in calculation. "On another matter, Mistress Roya, I understand that you and your mother and your grandmother hosted the women of the village after the burial of Alia's daughter."

"We were trying to help Alia with her grief. The support of other women can be soothing in a time like she is going through."

"Yes, of course, the support and sympathy of the other women in the village," he says distractedly and then, again pulling on his beard, adds, "and of course nothing else being spoken or planned?"

"What do you mean, Mullah Aman? What else would you expect us women to be doing?"

"You and your mother have been known to speak against the powers of the village. Your Grandmother Uzra does not seem to be able to control the two of you."

"But Mullah Aman, what is there to control? We are poor women of this village, just trying to serve Allah and wait for our father and brother to come home."

"Yes, yes you are waiting for your men to come home, but your interpretation on doing Allah's will may be different than I have taught."

"We are simple women, Mullah Aman. What is it we could misinterpret?"

"We will see, Mistress Roya. We will see. Please tell your grandmother I send my blessings." Then he turns and leaves.

Mullah Aman is a major powerbroker in this little huddle of homes. Mother and I continue to annoy him and the militia men. We need to do something before they address our distaste and rebellion against their will on us. I must speak with Mother. We must have a plan. He will be back for more small boys soon. Their scrutiny of us will increase.

Chapter 7:
FAHIMA—ALLAH SAVE THE CHILDREN

The heat is oppressive today. Sitting here under the old tree in the courtyard is cooler than being in the house, but there is not a breath of air. I had better put my Qur'an aside and go check on Mother Uzra. The dust is thick as snow and covering everything. An afternoon of quiet is unusual these days. The heat has driven everyone to shade and rest.

"Mother Uzra, are you well?"

"Fahima, I am weary from this heat, but feeling comfortable. The heat and humidity help the ache in my hands," comes the reply from the dark house.

"It is so stifling I was worried about you. You were so quiet in there."

"I am not moving much, but well for an old lady," she says with a little chuckle in her voice.

As I move into the house to see to Mother Uzra, a loud boom shakes everything. We both instinctually fall to the floor and cover our heads. I can hear falling debris and people running.

"Mother Uzra, are you alright?"

"Please help me off the floor. Can you tell where that was coming from?"

"Allah forbid, it sounds like it is coming from the school. Please sit here. I will run and check on Roya."

I need to cover my head and hurry to the school to make sure Roya and her students are all right. Everyone seems to be running in that direction. There is a dark cloud of smoke right where the school is. I must hurry.

A crowd has gathered at the back of the school where a small stand of trees used to be. Now there is a charred hole in the ground and small amounts of blood spattered on the uncharred earth around one end of the hole and tufts of singed black hair scattered on top of the wood debris like sooty snow.

I see Roya crying and huddled over something.

"Roya, are you alright daughter?"

"Yes Mother, but one of my students was playing back here and stepped on a landmine. It was Yasmine, Fawigia's ten-year-old daughter. One of her legs is severely maimed and her beautiful thick black hair is charred and patches are missing, but her face and skull were not damaged. She is unconscious and being tended by her mother."

"Now Fawigia has a wounded child. This village is not safe. Must we all sacrifice life and limb? It seems no one is spared." I wrap my arms around my own waist to help contain my distress.

"Let's hope she gets to keep the leg. Right now, it looks like Zalmai's did two months ago when he stepped on a landmine. He was not so lucky. Mother, I do not know if I can take much more of this. My students are so endangered I can barely focus on teaching them. I am so nervous about their safety. Who would put a landmine behind a school where children could be playing? I do not know why Yasmine was back here, but she has a right to expect it to be safe."

"Roya, there is no right of safety for our children in this village. There is no safe passage. No safe havens. Our village is a war zone."

Roya begins to sob into my shoulder. Fawigia and her family are carrying Yasmine to Fawigia's grandfather's truck and will drive her fifty-four miles to the closest doctor. As they pass, Roya grabs Yasmine's hand, "Yasmine, I promise you will feel better and be back in class soon. Allah be with you."

The girl looks at Roya groggily, blood smeared across her face, and tries to smile. A lock of thick, wavy black hair falls across her forehead as she closes her wet black eyes and passes out again. Her grandfather nods and continues to the waiting truck.

"I hope Allah allows that beautiful child to keep her leg. I better get back to your grandmother and let her know what has happened."

As I walk back to the house with Roya, Maky runs up.

"Fahima, wait, I need to talk to you. You too, Roya," Maky has Jalil on one hip, but Noor is nowhere to be seen.

"Maky, may Allah bless you. I hope all is well. Is it something with Ahmad?"

Maky shifts Jalil to her other hip and nervously whispers, "May we speak in your home and not here on the street?"

"Of course. Do you want to follow me now or meet me there a little later?"

"I would like to come once it is dark out and the children are asleep."

"That would be fine. I will expect you this evening then," I refrain from touching Maky's shoulder or the child and turn quickly, hoping no one noticed we spoke.

Roya and I hurry back to our home to check on Mother Uzra and pour some tea to settle our nerves. These continued acts of disruption and violence are getting more unsettling as the numbers mount. The emotional toll they take on each of us is sapping the energy and hope from us all. Waiting. Worrying. Crying. Grieving. This is no way to live. Mother Uzra knows the price we pay. She is right about the need to remove ourselves from this place, our home.

"Roya," I try to cheer her and wrap my arm around her shoulder as we walk. "She will survive. Yasmine is alive and, even if she loses that leg, life can be good for her."

"Mother, you are kind to try and cheer me, but we both know the reality of it. Growing up in this village is a death sentence. A sentence to a life of fear, disrespect, and mayhem. How do I teach my students to prepare for that?"

"Let's have tea. Maky wishes to speak with us tonight after the sun is down. Let's prepare dinner, clean up, and wait for her."

We walk the rest of the way to our home in silence.

Chapter 8:
KASHAR—WHY WE FIGHT

Militia Encampment

"Kill them, eat them, and clean up the mess," is my command to a cluster of my militiamen making the time pass by cock fighting. Better to eat those roosters then let them destroy one another.

"Farid, send Zalmai and Ahmad to see me under the shade of that tree." I point to an old tree, the hulks of two burned-out personnel carriers just outside the shade of the lower branches. It offers both shade and protection.

"Yes, Kashar."

"Farid, also bring me some tea."

"Yes, Commander."

"We need to go to the village of Washir for more supplies. In two days, a delivery of ammunition and more rifles will arrive from Qandahar. Where are my sons?"

"Father," says Ahmad as he walks into the shade of the tree, "here is the tea you asked of Farid."

"Where is your brother?"

"He is coming. He was cleaning his Kalashnikov and needed to put it back together first."

"Our equipment is old and the dust and heat wear them down. How about you? Have you cleaned your weapon lately?"

"Of course, Father. I am not a child; I am a militiaman. It is part of my duties."

"Zalmai, have you completed maintaining your weapon?" *As my youngest son walks up into the shade to join us, I notice he still has a noticeable limp that slows him. The shrapnel he took in his right leg when he was eighteen still cripples him. This fighting takes a more lasting toll on the young then an old man like me.*

"Sons, I need you to go to Washir and gather supplies. We need more food and water. We will get a new shipment of weapons from Qandahar the day after tomorrow, so I need to stay here. Take five men and have the villagers send food. Get water in Geresk. Take two of the pickups. Be watchful, reports tell us there is a splinter band of Taliban that just went through Lashkargah, believed to be on their way to Quetta to be resupplied in Pakistan."

"Of course, Father," says Ahmad. "Do we know how many Taliban are in that band?"

"There have been ten to twelve spotted by the villagers, but as we know there could be more in the shadows."

"Should we eliminate them before we get supplies?" questions Zalmai.

"Zalmai, young one, you are always ready for a fight. If they are on their way to Pakistan, let them go."

"But Father, what if they rearm and return?"

"If they do, we will deal with them then. If they are on their way out of our country without firing bullets, that is a victory for us. Let us just believe they are not going to punish our villagers on their way out."

"We can't be sure of that," adds Ahmad.

"No, we cannot, but we have to pick our fights. There are many enemies to defend against."

"Father, the school children's immunization will take place in Quandahar in two weeks. Will we go there to ensure all is safe?" Ahmad notes.

"Ah, that is one time even the Taliban honors a truce. Can we trust our enemies not to take revenge on our women and children at that time? They are unpredictable when it comes to observing traditions. Once we get new supplies and arms we will decide whether to go or not."

"So many fronts to protect, right Father?"

"You are right, Zalmai. This is also harvest time for the opium, so Walizada will be around with his men looking to get his product to continue to fund his business. When they come to extract their goods from the villages, they can do more harm than the Taliban. The heroin trade keeps our people in chains to the drug dealers and the drugs. The drug lords hold good people hostage with their money and violence."

"Our people pay twice. They pay the drug dealers with their field product and food and their girls, then they fund us to protect them with their money and food and, regrettably, sometimes with their girls. Father, are we really making things better?"

"Ahmad, that is the question. I have spent most of my adult life fighting someone. First the Russians, then the Taliban, always the drug dealers and warlords. There are so many fronts. So many enemies. So many lives lost."

"Even our mother," quickly adds Zalmai.

"War takes. It is indiscriminate. We try to protect our loved ones and sacrifice those who chose to fight, but war does not obey the rules. It will take the innocent as well."

"I fight to avenge my mother," says Zalmai.

"Brother, we fight because we know nothing else," corrects Ahmad.

"We fight for our dignity and to preserve our way of life," I remind my sons. "When our way of life becomes fighting, something must remind us what life was before. Remembering our loved ones grounds us to a better way."

"It also makes us bitter," Ahmad adds.

"One can take over the other, Ahmad," I tell them both. "Defending loved ones and seeking justice for their deaths after so many years turns into pure survival and revenge. In the day-to-day struggling, we lose sight of the real reason we are doing this. Fighting and anger become a way of life and we know no other."

"When will the fight finish, Father?" Zalmai finally questions.

"I do not know, son. All I know is we must continue to work against those who seek to change the way of life we used to know. I do not want life as it is now for you both to be the only life you know. Always fighting, always watching your back, constantly falling asleep with anger and hatred at the end of the day is not the way to live life according to Allah. We do this to protect our way of life and get back to it before those who wish to change it take us over."

"I look forward to the day when I can marry and have children and come home to my wife in peace," says Zalmai.

"One day my son, you shall. This I promise, if it takes my last breath. Allah be willing. Now, both of you go. We must continue this work until that day is here."

"Yes, Father."

"Yes, Kashar."

Chapter 9:
ROYA—ESCAPING THE SCHOOL OF MALICE

Evening prayers and dinner are over, and Mother and I are out in the courtyard in the cool of the night drinking our tea when Maky quietly slides in the side gate.

Mother says, "Please, Maky, let's go inside. It is warmer inside, but more private." She motions for Maky to lead the way into the house.

Once seated on the floor around the circular table, Maky drops her head covering and speaks.

"Fahima, Roya, Mullah Aman has come to inform me that Noor is to go to the madrassa at the beginning of next semester with three other boys from the school. He thinks Noor is very bright and wants to take him earlier than some of the others because he needs to begin learning his lessons."

"Mullah Aman's madrassa teachings are very different than what I teach," I note indignantly.

"Roya, please," says Mother. "You know what lessons he is talking about. Under the guise of the Qur'an they start early with these young male minds, brainwashing them to fight the infidels and sacrifice their lives for the Jihad. I'd like Mullah Aman to show me where in my Qur'an, the real word of Allah, where it says young boys should strap on explosives and kill other people in the name of Allah."

"I do not want Noor to go," Maky says, almost whispering.

"Oh Maky, I can understand how you feel. I do not know what to do to prevent it. Do we hide him? Where? Do we refuse to let him go? How do we secure him here?"

"Mother, we could hide him out at Hawa's farm."

"No, Roya, they would find him eventually and then seek revenge on Maky, Ahmad, and Hawa and her family."

"We could fake his death. We could set off a landmine, and say he was killed and there is no small body to even document it."

"Roya, those things would never work, and the retribution Mullah Aman and the militia would seek on us would be terrible."

"Mother, Maky can't just hand him over."

"Fahima, I am not brave. I am fearful for my Jalil, Ahmad, and myself. That is why I am here."

"Maky," says Mother, "this issue has been plaguing our village for a while now. Mothers keep losing their small sons to the Mullah and his madrassas. Roya loses students every year to the Mullah and his school. What can we do?"

"Mother, the time for immunizations is coming up soon. Do you think we could put Mullah Aman off until Noor has his immunizations? That would give us a little more time to think of something. After we return from Qandahar for the vaccinations, we could have a plan ready."

"Things do ease up to allow the children to travel and get their shots. I'm not sure Mullah Aman would think that getting vaccinated is significant enough to let Noor stay here. Still, what do we do when we return?"

"Maybe on the way he steps on a landmine and is killed. Not for real, Maky. Just a fake to let Mullah Aman think Noor is gone."

Maky chews on her index fingernail and then her lower lip. "I don't know. I am not very good at deception."

"You could do it for Noor, right?" I plead.

"Child," says Mother, "we will need a bigger deception then that to fool Mullah Aman. And now that I think about it, if we are going to devise a grand deception, we might as well save more than just one small boy."

"What are you thinking, Mother?" I ask astonished at what I think she is contemplating.

"Your grandmother believes you and I need to leave this village to save ourselves. If we are going to go, I couldn't leave without taking others with us. It is very risky and very dangerous, but these are desperate times. After Yasmine's accident today, it is clear our children are in extreme danger just going to school. Our boys are being ferried off to schools that teach malice and hate. We cannot wait for your father and brother to return. We must act to save ourselves and the children."

"Fahima, does that mean you will try to save Noor from the madrassa? Ahmad and I would be forever in your debt if you could." Maky leans over to hug Mother and begins to cry. "Fahima, we would owe you everything if you could do this."

Mother pats Maky on the back while still in her embrace and says, "This act will require all your strength and courage. We will be deceiving and standing up to men that do not like women to have an opinion or act on their own."

"It is about time we stood up for ourselves and our children," I say and join Maky in hugging Mother. When I look at Mother's face, she has a serious and drained look. "Mother, are you alright?"

"Roya, I do not know what Allah wants me to do, but I do know He wants us to save the children. I will pray that He will show me the way and protect us as we do this. We must all pray for wisdom and courage. Maky, go home to your children and pray. Do not breathe a word of this to anyone. Do you understand? Not a word to anyone. This could blow up before it begins if Mullah Aman gets word of our plan. We all know we have neighbors that would love to carry a story like ours to the Mullah for recognition. Information selling is a big business in this village. We don't have a lot of time to pull everything together. We must be smart and efficient."

"I am frightened, Fahima," says Maky, "But I trust you. I will pray for all of us." Maky grabs both of Mother's hands and kisses the tops of them. "Thank you, a million times, for saving my Noor."

"Please, Maky," cautions Mother, "We are not there yet. Go now to your sleeping children. Understand that you cannot write to Ahmad about this. If we must, we will figure another way to let him know what we are going to do. For now, we must just keep with one another. Roya, that goes for you too."

"I understand, Mother."

"Alright, let us get some sleep and start this planning fresh in the morning."

"Good night, Fahima and Roya. May Allah see that you sleep safe and well."

"Good night, Maky, the same to you," and Mother and I walk her to the side gate.

As we walk back to the house, Mother lets out a big sigh and leans her head on my shoulder.

"My Roya, I think we have just shouldered something that is going to be bigger than we are."

"Mother, we are strong, smart women. I believe Allah has picked us for his work."

"We shall see, darling. We shall see."

Chapter 10:
UZRA—THE PRODIGAL DAUGHTER RETURNS

Fahima, Roya, and I are having our morning tea when we hear the sound of trucks rolling through the village. This means the militia is on the move and could be at our door looking for food.

"Fahima, do you hear that?" I ask.

"Yes, Mother Uzra, the militia is moving through. Only Allah knows why and what they might want from us. Let us stay quiet and hope we do not get a knock at the door."

Roya pours more tea and we sit in silence eating our fruit and bread and hoping they pass through without incident—although that rarely happens. Generally, they come through looking for informers, new recruits, or supplies. *I am not sure why they come here looking for supplies—we have so very little to offer. I don't know what they think we are hiding. Bullets under our blankets?*

A truck stops at the house next door. We are silent. We hear footsteps and the squeak of the side gate opening.

"Oh, Mother, they are in the courtyard," Roya whispers.

We continue to sit as silently as we can. All three of us are breathing that short pant of nervous fear. Then a soft knock comes at the side door from the courtyard to the house.

"Do we answer it, Mother?" Roya gasps in a nervous push of air.

"If it were the militia, they would have no problem coming to the front door. I am guessing this is not them," Fahima reassures her.

"Fahima, I agree with you. Please go see who is there."

Fahima gets up and quietly moves to the side door, listens a moment, asks who is there, and then flings it open to find Monisa, my great niece standing there.

"Monisa, come in child. How did you get here? Why are you here?" I ask.

"Great Aunt Uzra, Cousin Fahima, Cousin Roya, thank you for letting me in. I am here from Kabul."

"All this way, child."

"Yes, Great Aunt. I was living in Kabul, but things are getting too crazy and violent there, so I thought coming here would be safer."

"Monisa, we are so happy to see you are safe and well," says Fahima as she leads Monisa to the table and reaches for another cup to pour tea.

Roya rises and hugs Monisa, then says, "Monisa, tell me of Kabul. It has been so long since I was working there. I so miss the city life."

"Roya," Monisa begins, "things are very different in Kabul now. The Taliban has completely reversed our way of life there. We must cover in those ridiculous burqas. We are not allowed to work out of the home. We must be escorted by male family members when in public. We can't even wear white shoes."

At that we all laugh.

"More importantly, there are constant car bombs and shootings and explosions. I lost a very good co-worker last week that was in the market with her brother when a suicide bomber blew himself up.

She was standing within five feet of the bomber and it killed her. Her brother was on the other side of her and he lost an arm and one eye."

"But Monisa, I thought you weren't allowed to work," questions Roya.

"As you know, I am a hairdresser. I work in a shop with three other women. Who are our customers? The wives and women of the Taliban. Other women are not allowed to have their hair done, but the women of the Taliban do. What hypocrisy! I had to flee because one of my customers overheard me talking about the lunacy of the Taliban's mandates and she told her husband."

"So Monisa, you were in danger?" Fahima asks.

"Oh, Cousin, I was in big trouble. Luckily one of my other clients loved the way I did her hair and I guess she liked me. Her husband out ranked the tattle teller's, so I was allowed to hitch a ride here with this group coming through town."

"Is the group currently in town part of Kashar's militia?" Roya probes.

"No," explains Monisa. "This group is from Kabul. They have an American attachment and are looking for stolen weapons and drugs. I could only go with a group that had Americans in it. The Afghanistan men would not tolerate me being with them."

"Monisa that is very dangerous, but very exciting," Roya noted with a hint of envy in her voice.

"I have learned you have to do what you have to do to survive," Monisa says offhandedly.

"Child," I say, "your whole life has been a dangerous adventure."

"You are right, Great Auntie. Somehow, I always choose to take the path less traveled and get in trouble for my selection," Monisa grins and shakes her head in frustration.

"Monisa," asks Fahima, "Did you ever make amends with your family for running off with that Russian soldier? Did they forgive you?"

"Cousin Fahima, you know forgiveness for something like that is not the way of my father and certainly not my brothers. Mother understood but was powerless against the men in my family to save me from my banishment. At least they didn't kill me for the shame they imagined I brought on them. Do you consider me a blight on the family?"

"We consider you a desperately in love young woman who followed her heart and not the will of her family," I say.

"That's why I came to you today. Great Aunt Uzra, you always seemed to be forgiving and understanding. My grandmother, your sister, could not even take me in in my time of need."

"My sister Jamilla is still haunted by her inability to comfort you during that time. She would be pleased that you felt you could come here to us," I explain.

"Yes, you can join my mother amongst the ranks of those who disturb Afghani men with their acts of defiance," adds Roya. "Right, Mother?"

"Yes, Roya, it looks like Monisa and I are both on the uninvited list for militia events."

All four of us laugh.

Chapter 11:
ROYA—TICKING CLOCK

"Monisa, you have had a long journey. Please take some time to clean up and rest. When you are ready, let's catch up. It has been several years since we have had time to talk."

"I feel really grimy after riding in the back of that military truck and probably look terrible," admits Monisa as she runs her hand down her wavy, dark hair and over her cheeks. "I'll wash up, change clothes, and take a little nap, and then I should be more presentable and ready to fill you in on the missing chapters of my crazy life." She smiles, shakes her head, and adds, "I am a walking television show. Stay tuned, as they say, and I will be back to fill you in."

"I have to go teach, so I will see you later today. I'm sure Grandmother and Mother will take good care of you." We embrace and I turn to pick up my bag and leave. "Goodbye, Mother. Goodbye, Grandmother. I will see you this afternoon when I return."

"Allah be with you, Roya," says Grandmother.

As I gather my teaching materials I am thinking, *I am anxious today to see if Yasmine is back in class and how she is doing after her explosion injury. She did lose the leg just above her knee and I hear she has been fitted with a metal artificial leg. She is young and healthy, praise Allah, and hopefully will adjust quickly to her new way of life. She is such a bright student. I do hope she is brave enough and strong enough to get to class. Her education is even more important to her now that she has a disability.*

What is this pile in my way? It looks like some of the debris left from the explosion that took Yasmine's leg. I really should clean that up. It is a sad reminder of that violent day. As I grab the knob to open the school door, I can hear the eager voices and the laughter of the children arriving for class. *Such happy sounds. In the village there is not much happiness, and the sounds of pure childish joy make me think for a brief second that life is back to normal.* Noor comes to greet me, and then I look up at my desk and see Mullah Aman surveying the room as he waits for me to arrive.

"Mistress Roya, may Allah be with you this fine morning," he says over the chatter of the children. "This is a fine-looking class you have today."

"Allah be with you, Mullah Aman. Yes, it is a fine morning and it seems everyone is here eager to learn," I reply.

"I see our little lady who had the unfortunate accident is here and returning to her studies. Praise Allah, He saved her from that untimely mishap," Mullah Aman turns his focus to the back of the room where Yasmine is sitting with two other girls her age, whispering to one another. She has her skirt lifted to her knee to show her friends her new metal leg, but quickly pulls it down when they notice Mullah Aman looking their way.

"Yasmine is a very bright student," I turn and smile at her and nod my head. "I am thankful to Allah also that He spared her life and she is brave enough to return to school and complete her education, Mullah Aman."

"Yes, Mistress Roya, girls' educations are a pleasure to Allah," he says as he strokes his long gray beard.

"And we are all thankful to you, Mullah Aman, that Allah has shown you the value of educating girls and allowed them to attend school in this village. For this we truly thank Allah and you," I bow my head in respectful acknowledgement, as he would expect.

"And how are our young men doing these days?"

"The small ones that we have are always a challenge. It seems the boys do not like to sit still as readily as the girls do," I answer, subtly noting to him that the older boys are not here, he has taken them all to the madrassa.

"Of course, you realize, Mistress Roya, that Allah has a separate educational plan for the boys," he says pronouncing separate slowly for emphasis.

I would like to debate him on the need for a separate educational plan for the boys, but cannot risk losing his good will right now. "They do settle down and get to their studies Mullah Aman, but it does take a little more patience with them," I answer.

"Indeed. Well, in the madrassa there is more discipline and they are expected to focus on their studies more intently."

Shooting guns and making bombs does require more intense study, I think, but smile and agree with Mullah Aman with a slight nod of my head. *What can one say?* Then without thinking I say, "Mullah, you do realize these children, all of them, need to go to be vaccinated in a couple of weeks."

"Yes, Mistress Roya, I am aware of that. Before the boys go to madrassa, they do need their vaccinations. After that time they can change schools."

What have I done? We have no plan to leave, but it seems Mullah does plan to come for Noor and the other small boys for the madrassa after they are vaccinated. I must tell Mother that we need a plan and we need it now or Noor and the others will be taken, as the boys before them were.

"Well, good day Mistress Roya, I shall leave you to your pupils and their lessons. May Allah be with you," Mullah turns and waits for me to bow and acknowledge his blessing and slowly walks to the door, again stroking his beard and looking at the group of small boys, including Noor, sitting near the window laughing and jostling one another.

I take a deep breath, paste a smile on my face, and turn to begin my day of instruction.

Chapter 12:
FAHIMA—TIME FOR ACTION

"Monisa, would you like more tea? Roya should be home very soon and you won't have to spend the rest of your day talking to old ladies," I say as I get up from where we have been talking to reheat the water so it will be ready when Roya comes home from school.

"Cousin Fahima, it is just nice to be in a friendly, family home for a change," says Monisa. "I have been in Kabul so long and so far away from my family that I have forgotten how nice it can be."

"It is good to see you and know that Allah has protected you in all your, shall we say travels ," Mother Uzra adds. "Your stories of Kabul and what is going on there are as terrible, but more colorful, than we can add of life here."

"I didn't realize that way out here in the villages things were as intense as they are in the city. It seems nowhere is safe and peaceful anymore," notes Monisa.

"You are too young to remember the peaceful times, "I say. "As I have said to Roya many times, there was a time in Afghanistan when we were progressing like the rest of the world and women were beginning to be allowed to be our full selves. That is all gone now."

"I do know some, Cousin Fahima. One of the things that attracted me to Sergio, my Russian love, was the hope of a life in his country where women are better regarded. I was so young and so idealistic. I really thought with him I could break through this male-dominated life and become my full self with him. I did not realize my own family did not wish the same for me."

The front door opens and Roya arrives home from school.

"Roya, how was your day?" I say as I help her set her bag down and direct her to sit with us for tea.

"Mother, we must complete our plan and execute it. Mullah Aman was again at school asking about the boys. I am so sorry, but I mentioned that the boys need to go and be vaccinated before they go to the madrassa. I hope I haven't spoken too soon or said too much. I am so distressed."

"Darling, it will be fine. We don't have a plan, just an idea right now, so you couldn't possibly have given anything away. Besides, Mullah Aman knows very well when and where the vaccinating takes place."

"I am so nervous, I don't want to do anything to jeopardize these children. My stomach is in knots. I am so fearful," Roya says as she wrings her hands with nervous energy.

"What's going on?" interrupts Monisa.

"Monisa, the village mullah gathers up the young boys of Roya's school and moves them to the madrassas, supposedly religious school for boys. These schools are really training centers for the militias, teaching the young ones radical religious beliefs and how to shoot a gun and make bombs. Even more grotesquely, it teaches them why they should die for the Jihad in the name of Allah."

"Well," says Monisa, "some things never change. Not being around children and families I didn't know that was happening, but it doesn't surprise me. I've seen those little soldiers around Kabul. There are boys barely big enough to shoulder their gun running behind their leaders, barely big enough to keep up with man-size steps. What a sight!"

"Monisa, you speak of family," I say. "One of our own is about to be taken. Do you remember Maky and Ahmad? Their son Noor is on Mullah Aman's list to be taken soon. Maky has pleaded with us to find a way to save him."

"Noor is a really bright little guy," adds Roya. "We cannot stand to see him sucked into this world of violence and religious fervor."

"I get it," says Monisa. "What do you plan to do to save him?"

"We don't have a plan yet," I admit. "And it's not just about Noor. We need to save all the little ones. We need to save ourselves. Monisa, our men are gone. We women are left as unprotected, disrespected baggage, not allowed to do anything but supply the needs of the militia. Taking Noor is the last straw. One of our young girls lost a leg stepping on a landmine outside the school. The school. Our children are not safe. We women are not safe. I believe Allah wants us to find our own way. The question is how?"

"Cousin Fahima, that is certainly a tall order," Monisa comments in astonishment as she rejoins the other three women at the table. "You have so few resources here. Besides, your movements are under a microscope. At least in Kabul we had some ability to move around undetected. Those required burqas were a handy disguise. I am the queen of deception. How can I help? What will you do?"

"We had some thought of sweeping the children and ourselves away under the guise of taking them to Quandahar for their vaccinations. The when is already set, as the vaccinations will begin in two weeks. The how is still not thought out. I suppose we can gather as women to plan the journey together. Typically, each family travels on their own. I am not sure we could even get away as one group of women and children. Then there's the issue of a male chaperone. Who do we use that is sympathetic to our cause and willing to jeopardize himself for the effort? This is a huge, very dangerous endeavor."

"That is a crazy idea, Cousin Fahima," marvels Monisa. "Really crazy. I love it! Finally, some women doing something about their plight. I'm in. "

"Oh Monisa, I hate to draw you into our conspiracy," I say.

"Monisa, your grandmother would never forgive me if I allowed you to enter into yet another rebellious act that threatens your safety," Mother Uzra blurts out.

"How can you stop me, Great Aunt Uzra?" Monisa responds with a devilish grin.

"You really thrive on this rebellion stuff, don't you Monisa?" Roya laughs as she sips her fresh cup of tea.

"It's kind of the road my life has taken," Monisa replies. "It seems I'm always at odds with the way things are being done or what I am expected to do."

"No question about that, Monisa," I add. "Okay, so we are four conspirators. How do we construct and implement a plan?"

"Besides Noor, we need to determine who else we are going to save and if their mothers are committed to this life-changing effort. Because, make no mistake, this will change the lives of all that participate," proffers Roya. "Once we leave there is no coming back, and we are all in danger."

"This is overwhelming," I sigh. "This act requires tremendous faith and superb planning and deception. We are not used to executing this kind of enormous plan. I feel so inadequate."

"Mother, you are very smart. This is a game we learn as we go along. We can do this. We have to do this to salvage the lives of our little ones and for ourselves," Roya puts her arm around my shoulders and draws me to her. "We have to at least try. What we have now is not worth suffering through. We must take the initiative for our own futures."

"I agree," adds Monisa. "As young women, our futures are not bright. Both Roya and I do not have children yet, and right now I would not wish to. This world is too violent and evil for a child of mine. Even my child—the child of Monisa, the great rebel!" She rises from her chair and pumps her fist in the air like a triumphant athlete. "Cousin Fahima, I love you even more for even considering doing this. We must all take responsibility if we are to change the ways of our country."

"Not all the mothers will agree," cautions Roya.

"If they don't, then they carry the guilt of not doing everything they could to improve the future of their children," Monisa emphatically interjects.

"Okay, girls," I rise to calm them. "We know what we have to do. Let's figure out what it is we are going to do. Roya, please tell Jahan to come by this evening after dark. Also Maky and Aunt Sakina. Please tell them to leave the children at home. We have to be as quiet and unnoticed as possible."

"Yes, Mother."

"All right, let's get this thing together," Monisa joyfully exclaims.

Mother Uzra sits, silently sipping her tea. I need to understand her thinking as we proceed.

Chapter 13:
FAHIMA—THE QUEST BEGINS

Our small home is full of murmuring women. Prayer rugs accommodate frightened, expectant women anxious for change, somehow, to their base existence. We must be quiet and not draw attention from the outside. The militia is camped at the edge of town. If we are too loud, they will come to investigate. If we are found plotting an escape, Kashar will make even the children pay for our daring. *Are we brave enough? Is Allah willing to help us?* With a deep breath and a smile, I begin.

"As Roya has informed you, vaccinations will be given in two weeks in Quandahar. My proposal is to take the children for their vaccinations, but not return here. Instead, we will travel on with them and seek somewhere to hide. This is an easy plan for me to propose since my children are already grown and not at risk."

"Fahima, again I implore you to lead us and help us save our children," pleads Maky. "Sakina and I are asking you to endanger yourself and Roya, but without your skills and intelligence we cannot do this."

"Fahima and I," says Jahan softly, interrupting Maky, "have had lives outside this village. We know it is hard for you who have not to imagine what the world can be, but there are gentler, better places to raise children that are not given to violence and angry rage. The best solution to this problem would be to convince the men to put their arms down and to stop being angry and suspicious of everyone's intentions and religion. That is a long, hard process that will not end if children grow up to continue that way of thinking and feed their ranks."

"Our best hope is to take the coming generation away from this life and show them a better way. I say this knowing that I will never live to see that happen, but I am beseeching my best friend and sister Fahima to help you all accomplish that. Build a place where you mothers are in control and allowed to teach and show your children a more peaceful, respectful way to live and honor Allah."

"Jahan," I say, "I will do this for my beloved friend and all those children who are part of my family, village, and country. Tonight we begin our ascent to a higher plane of living for ourselves and for our children. Maybe by example the men will see how harmful their thinking and way of doing things has become. How far from Allah they have strayed, despite their fervent insistence that the world around them are all infidels. We must make them realize some value in our gender. They do not see the irony and destruction in their actions."

"Mother, you and Jahan are right," adds Roya. "We all need to ascend to a more civilized plateau of living. My generation can no longer tolerate the decline our country has taken to a more primitive way of life and violent means of resolving perceived injustices. Women in other countries have shown the way. We can, too."

Sitting next to Mother Uzra is Sakina. She stands and says, "Fahima, we look to you to help us save our children and ourselves. What is it you wish us to do?"

"To be successful, we must keep our numbers to something manageable," I instruct. "Our first official move is to define the group and to swear each to secrecy. We must keep our plans from those we love to make this work. Is that agreed?"

In the room are Jahan, Roya, Monisa, Maky, Sakina, and Fawigia, Yasmine's mother. Each think for a minute about the true meaning of my words and then all nod their heads in the affirmative. Jahan rises slowly and asks that we each pray to Allah to send His wisdom and protection to us in this endeavor. After our prayers, we begin the detailed discussions of how we will proceed.

It is now late into the night. As Roya and I clean up the cups and plates silently, I run through my mind what our band of rebels looks like. First is young mother Maky and her toddler Jalil and the focus of our attention, Noor.

Sakina, my sister-in-law, will be with us and so will my two teenage nieces, Shafika and Nooria. Roya and Monisa are the young, strong women we will certainly need. Roya has included Yasmine's family – her mother Fawigia which will mean her two small brothers and little sister. I wish it could be every child in the village, but if we hope to be successful we must keep our band manageable and, more importantly, less noticeable as we travel.

A crucial element to this plan is who will be our male escort? We cannot move from town to town and across the country without a male chaperone. Who in the world can we trust?

Chapter 14:
FAHIMA—WHO WILL BE OUR MALE ESCORT?

"Mother Uzra, who do you think we can use as our male chaperone?" As we sip our morning tea, I think out loud.

"There are not a lot of candidates, Fahima, with most of the able-bodied men gone to the militia or out of town working. Your Uncle Wardak is too old and would never make the trip. Cousin Yaqub, we think, is working with the drug dealers, so he would not be reliable."

"Oh Mother Uzra, it would be so perfect if Rahmat or Ghulam were here to accompany us. Many things would be better if Rahmat and Ghulam were here."

"Yes, having your husband and grown son would certainly make things better, but that would be the case for the whole village. If all the husbands and grown sons were back, things would be very different."

"Well, who do we have? Ahmad's uncle Khair might do."

"Fahima, he is too fragile and would never make the journey. You need someone strong and young. There are not many of those still here."

"You are right. Who is still around?" As I finish my tea, the day I ran into Hawa at the well comes to mind. "You know, Mother Uzra, who has young men still at home? Hawa. Her sons have been allowed to stay and work the poppies. They are good young men. If we encounter drug dealers, they will allow him to travel. Kashar and the militia know he is not available to them for the militia because of the drug dealers. If we meet the Taliban, he will simply be a male chaperone. I hate to drag Hawa into our rebellion, but she, too, could be a big help."

"Fahima, that is a very good idea. You are asking Hawa and Omar to send off one of their sons on a very dangerous journey, one that could easily get him killed or imprisoned. But I suppose working for drug lords is not without its dangers also."

"I hate to expose our plan to yet another, but if Hawa is agreeable that would be the solution to our chaperone. I need to negotiate with Hawa and Omar anyhow, to get extra food to feed our traveling band of rebels."

"I suspect there are a variety of things you will need from Omar and Hawa that we do not have here in the village, Fahima."

"You are right, Mother Uzra. We have some unique needs to launch this escape plan." We laugh.

"What do you need me to do to help?"

"You need to be the center of communication for Rahmat and Ghulam. I cannot let them know before we leave what we are doing. When they return, you are the unwritten communication of our plan. I know you will not know exactly where we are, but at least you can tell them our destination and, of course, why we have left."

"I'm sure Rahmat will understand why you left immediately."

"I am very fearful of leaving and never seeing my husband and son again. On the other hand, I could stay here and never see them again too."

"Fahima, you must have faith that Allah will work all of this out. In your heart, you are trying to do the right thing. That will be recognized and rewarded. Of that, I am sure."

"I wish I was as sure as you are, Mother Uzra. My stomach has been in a knot since we began this adventure."

"Good morning, Mother. Is it time for prayers?" says Roya joining them..

"Soon, darling. How did you sleep?"

"Not well, Mother. Until we are out of here and safe somewhere else, I will not sleep sound."

"I know, Dear. I know."

Chapter 15:
UZRA—ONE SON

It is a somber day, thinks Uzra while she folds and replaces her prayer rug on the neat pile in the corner of the small room that faces west to Mecca. *Fahima has gone to check on Jahan and take her some food. Poor Jahan grows weaker and weaker every day. This business of the flight worries her, as all of us, and drains her strength. Roya is at school hoping Mullah Aman will not descend upon her again, and Monisa is meeting with a distant cousin. I do hope Monisa is discreet and does not reveal our plans. This is a small village, but some have very large noses. I'll brew a cup of tea to help take the ache out of my knees and hands. Fahima should be back soon.*

There is a soft sound at the side door. "Fahima, is that you?"

"No, grandmother, it is me, Ghulam," comes an even softer voice from the open door.

"Ghulam! My prayers have been answered. You are home," Uzra says as she rushes to hug him. Then she stops short. Looking at his legs and deeply bruised face, she realizes he is badly wounded.

"Grandmother, it is so good to be home and see you. Where is Mother?" he asks as he scans the room, looking for Fahima.

"What has happened? Why are you here?" Uzra asks almost too cautious to really know why.

"I have been severely wounded, as you can see. Kashar sent me home since I am no use to him and he does not want to have to feed and care for me. This is how all badly injured militia are treated." Ghulam explains with a catch in his throat.

"How is your father? Where is Rahmat?" Uzra begs.

"Father is alright. He is not wounded as I. Kashar is using him as his accountant, therefore he does not have to fight as we young ones do." Ghulam struggles to a chair in the kitchen to sit down.

"Here, poor boy," says Uzra, rushing to help him and adjust the chair so he may be seated. "I have tea ready."

"That would be nice, Grandmother. I have been traveling all night. There are Taliban fighters hidden everywhere, so we must be careful in our travels," Ghulam says as he sips the warm tea.

"Here, let me add some honey," Uzra turns to a shelf and brings the honey jar down and adds a generous spoonful to Ghulam's tea. "This will nourish you and help you heal. What is the nature of your injuries?"

Ghulam looks down at his legs and the heavy bandages encircling the right. Then he quietly says, "I have shrapnel in my right leg. They wanted to amputate, but I would not allow it. I know it is festering and that could kill me, but I am not ready to lose it. I know there are women in the village who can do wonders with healing, so Kashar finally let me come home to seek medical attention, hoping I would heal and return to the fighting."

"Well," Uzra begins, "Jahan is the best at natural remedies, but she is very ill right now. Her cancer will soon overtake her despite all our prayers to Allah."

"I'm so sorry to hear that, Grandmother. Mother must be very upset about her best friend," Ghulam continues to sip his tea, and straightens his bandaged leg under the table for more comfort.

"Are you in a lot of pain, Ghulam?" Uzra asks, examining the bandage.

"Some, mostly from walking on it to get home. In camp we have plenty of morphine, but I have resisted taking too much because of the addiction. What I really need is antibiotics to kill the infection, and then to get those pieces of metal out."

"It seems if you walked here the leg is still useable."

"Yes Grandmother, it will hold me and I can walk on it, but with effort and an unsteady gait. But praise Allah I am alive and for now still have that leg. Too many of our men have lost limbs and worse to the landmines and self-designed bombs."

"When your mother returns, we must tend to that leg before you lose it, or we lose you."

"Thank you, Grandmother. I praise Allah that you, Mother, and Roya are here to help me. I am helpless on my own."

Uzra stands behind the chair and puts her arms around him and her head gently on the top of his head. "Of course we will do what we can, Ghulam," she says softly into the thick head of wavy hair she has watched grow from a baby.

More sounds at the door and Fahima rushes in, shouting Ghulam's name.

"Ghulam, Ghulam I have heard in the village that you are here." She rushes to him and squeezes him in her arms while he sits. She steps back to look him over, and her eyes scan onto the legs and the bandages.

"Oh, my son. I can imagine what happened. How bad is it?"

"Mother, praise Allah I can see you again. My leg is badly wounded as I have told Grandmother. They wanted to cut it off, but I talked Kashar into letting me seek help here in the village. He knows of Jahan's healing abilities and is hoping the leg will be saved and I can return to fight."

"Oh, Ghulam. How is your father?" Fahima asks, hesitant to know the truth.

"He is alright. Kashar is using him to keep account of the money, so he does not have to fight."

"Thank Allah," says Fahima as she continues down his body to check every aspect of his wounds.

"Fahima," begins Uzra. "How did you find Jahan today?"

"Mother, she is slipping away from us," Fahima reports with a soft, sad note in her voice. "Despite her attitude and her quiet suffering, she is being overcome by the cancer. Our prayers are not enough to save her. I feel so terribly helpless, as if I am letting her down."

"Daughter, cancer is an enemy we have no weapons for here in our primitive village. Even in Kabul there might not be enough medical wonders to save her from this."

"At least in Kabul they could keep her comfortable. She has resisted taking the opium for pain, but I'm not sure why."

"It is her faith, Fahima. That is why she does not take the opium. Right now her faith is all she has left."

"I suppose you are right, Mother Uzra."

Fahima is now kneeling at Ghulam's right leg. "Son, at the very least we must address this leg. Mother Uzra, we need to treat his injuries, but Allah may have answered our prayers and brought us our own chaperone for our journey to Quandahar."

Ghulam looks from mother to grandmother with a puzzled smile.

"Fahima," replies Uzra, "If we can get this young man healed, you are right. He is just what you need to complete the plan."

Chapter 16:
FAHIMA—LIFE'S TRAGIC BALANCE

"Ghulam, rest here," I help him move to a small cot to stretch out and support his injured leg. "Jahan cannot come, but I will ask her what to do and be back quickly. Mother Uzra, begin boiling water and please find clean fabric we can use to re-bandage him. I will see Jahan."

I leave them and hurry back to Jahan's home. She is too weak to come and help, but she can explain to me what to do.

"Fahima, you are back," Jahan says as I quietly re-enter her home.

"I'm so sorry to wake you, Jahan, but I need your help. Ghulam has returned and he is seriously injured." I describe his wounds and Jahan tells me what to do and directs me to a shelf to retrieve some powders she has stored there.

"Thank you, darling. Without your healing wisdom my son could lose his leg."

"Fahima," Jahan draws me close to where she is lying and whispers, "I am sorry I cannot do more for you. You and your family mean everything to me. Go. Go take care of your son. May Allah be with you."

I bend and gently kiss her on the forehead. "And you mean everything to us. I must go now. Please rest."

Jahan settles back onto her pallet, and I rush out to return home with the instructions and healing powders.

I find Ghulam on the cot, and Mother Uzra and Sakina tending him. He is moaning in pain and only half conscious.

"Mother Uzra, help me remove these soiled wrappings. Sakina, please bring the water and fabric over. Okay, Ghulam, here we go. This is Jahan's best advice."

An hour later, the three of us have successfully removed the metal, and cleaned all of the wounds and re-bandaged them. I give Ghulam a solution in his tea that Jahan says will kill infection and help him sleep.

"He seems to be more peaceful now," notes Sakina.

"Thank you for your help, Sakina," Mother Uzra adds. "Your young hands are a big help to Fahima. Mine are not as nimble. The two of you did a great job fishing out those slivers of metal tearing up Ghulam's flesh."

"It took all of us," I add. "And yes, your good hands and eyes really helped, Sakina."

"Mother Uzra, if you would keep an eye on him, I will try and find a ride out to Hawa's."

"Fahima," says Sakina, "Uncle Khair is here with his old truck to take Maky and little Jalil to clinic. Let's see if he will take you to Hawa's without asking too many questions. I think we can trust him."

"That's a good idea, Sakina. I'll be back as soon as I can, Mother Uzra."

"I will be fine with Ghulam, Fahima. Go."

"Okay, Sakina, let's find Maky and Uncle Khair. Allah be with you, Mother Uzra."

Three hours later, I return home to find Mother, Roya, Monisa, Sakina, Nooria, and Shafika gathered, getting ready for evening prayers.

"Fahima, you are back," says Mother Uzra.

"Yes, I spoke with Hawa, but on the way back a roadblock detained Uncle Khair and I. Why is everyone gathered here?"

Roya stands and moves to me. She puts both hands on my shoulders and looks at me with tears in her eyes.

"Mother, while you were gone Jahan went to Allah. I'm so sorry."

I stagger to sit in a chair. Roya moves next to me and puts her arm around my shoulders. I am in shock. *I just saw her hours ago. Jahan helped me save Ghulam's leg.* I knew her time was close, but this is too much for me to deal with all at once. Sakina and the girls kneel in front of me and express their sympathy. I cannot speak.

"Fahima," says Mother Uzra, "Allah has relieved her of her suffering. Her last act was to help you save Ghulam. I'm sure that gave her comfort."

"I know this is Allah's will, but he has taken my best friend when I needed her most," I say to Mother Uzra through my tears.

"Yes, that is true Fahima," Mother Uzra adds, "But it is His will. He has another plan for you."

"Mother," Roya comforts, "I'm sure Jahan did not want you worrying about her as we launch our big plan. She is at peace. I would think it will be a little easier for you to leave this village now."

"Of course you are right, Roya. But Jahan has always been there for me. I will be a wagon with one wheel missing now."

"Fahima," Sakina looks into my face with her sad eyes welled with tears and says, "She will always be with you. All the time you spent growing up together and going to college together, all those times are in your head and will never leave."

"You are all correct. It is just a shock to lose her right now. Let's all say our evening prayers and ask Allah to keep and care for her."

Each one wipes their eyes and gets a prayer rug to begin the nightly ritual. I check Ghulam, who is quietly sleeping before I kneel and begin my prayers.

Dear Allah, please show me the way to goodness and help me make the right decisions for our plan. Allow Jahan to watch over us and be proud of what we accomplish in her absence, but with her spirit always with us.

Chapter 17:
ROYA—VILLAGE GIRLS

The house is quiet. Mother is out again. Grandmother is resting and Ghulam is still unconscious on his pallet in the living room. Monisa and I are about to sit down with a cup of tea and really catch up on our lives. It has been so hectic since she arrived.

"Here, Monisa, let me pour you fresh tea."

"Thanks, Roya. It is finally a little settled here," Monisa notes as she carefully sips her tea.

"This is not normal for us. Although Mother is very connected to this village, these days everyone generally stays to themselves. There is very little entertaining. The women of the village cannot risk drawing attention," I explain with a tightening of my lips so as not to start on a tangent about how in despair we are.

"I see that. Things are only slightly better in Kabul and only because there are more people and more ways to hide." Monisa sets her cup down and looks at Ghulam, inanimate in his current state.

"Roya, you must be so glad to have your brother home and know that your father is not fighting."

"It is a complete blessing to have Ghulam here and to know of father. I have missed both of them so and worried that they might already be dead."

"You are so blessed to have loving and supportive men in your family. My brothers hate me. My father banished me. My brothers are not capable of honor killing me, but they cannot see beyond father's rage at my love for Sergio and the dishonor I have brought to the family."

"It must be very difficult for you, especially since you are the only girl in your family. I would guess that your mother is powerless to influence them in any way."

"Poor Mother is a prisoner in her own home. I feel guilty that I am not there to speak up for her and protect her, but if I were at home, it would be worse for her."

"Where is Sergio? Is he in Kabul?"

"No. His unit has returned to Moscow. The Taliban ran the Russians completely out. I have an address but have not communicated with him in more than a year. I haven't seen him in more than sixteen months. I miss him so. I still have hope we will be together some day, but that hope gets dimmer every month we are apart."

"Oh Monisa, your heart must be breaking." We touch hands on the table.

"I am strong and stubbornly optimistic. Someday Roya. Someday Sergio and I will be together."

Yet another knock comes at the door, and it carefully opens to reveal Nooria and Shafika, my teenage cousins.

"Hi, girls. What brings you here?" I ask.

Nooria, the youngest by two years, speaks, "Mother sent us to bring soup for Ghulam." Shafika is carrying a container wrapped in a worn towel. Clearly the soup is still hot.

"Ghulam will welcome this nourishment when he comes around. Come sit with Monisa and I. Would you like tea?"

"No tea for me," says Shafika as she places the soup carefully on the table. "It upsets my stomach without food."

"Well," I say, "we can find a little something to go with it."

"She always does this," replies Nooria with a hint of intolerance in her tone.

"I can understand that," Monisa says, trying to clear the air a little. "Sometimes that happens to me, too."

"How are you girls doing? You are both such good students. I enjoy having you in school," I say to change the subject.

"Our house is always sad, not having father here," Shafika says with downturned eyes. "Mother cries a lot."

I move to put my arm around Shafika's shoulder, "I know, darling. These are difficult times especially for growing and maturing young ladies like you both."

"Cousin Roya and Monisa, Shafika and I were wondering if you would tell us about Kabul and going to college?" Nooria asks boldly. Shafika pokes her and gives her a disapproving look. "We want to know about boys and life outside the village. Don't we Shafika?" She pokes her sister back.

Monisa and I smile and begin to chuckle. "Naturally you would be curious about boys. You have no brothers and haven't even grown up with older boys in school. At least Monisa I had that."

"All I can say is they are wonderful and awful at the same time," adds Monisa with a wink.

"I don't understand, Monisa," says Shafika.

"Oh, you will when you get the chance to be around them all grown up," Monisa advises.

"Mother says you had a Russian boyfriend in Kabul," Nooria eagerly probes.

"I did. He is still the love of my life. It is wonderful to be in love, and heartbreaking at the same time when you cannot be together."

"He sounds very handsome," Nooria says a little whispery. "Tell us about him."

"Yes, Monisa," I say. "I would like to hear that, too."

"Ah, my Sergio. He is tall, maybe four or five inches taller than I am. He has to bend a little to kiss me," Monisa adds with a melodramatic flare that she knows will stir the girls' fantasies. "He has blond hair like a lot of Russians, and blue eyes. He gets very tan when he is here in our weather, which makes his hair bleach out and his eyes an even more intense blue."

"How did you meet him?" the serious, probing Shafika asks.

"We were both in the market one day. I accidentally knocked over a basket of grapes and he very politely offered to help me pick them up. Of course, we could not speak to one another because I did not speak Russian and he only knew a little Arabic. In sign language, he offered to buy me a cup of coffee and I accepted. I was completely amazed at how cute he was. He was shy and very polite. I couldn't say no."

"Remember girls," I note, as always the teacher. "In those days, before the Taliban, you could be in the market alone and even have a cup of coffee with a strange man. These days that is certainly not allowed."

"You and Monisa sure had it good," Nooria interjects. "How are we ever to meet boys in these times?"

I nod in acknowledgement. "I know, girls. These are terrible times for growing up into young women and finding your true love. Fortunately for you two, our family does not believe in the old way of arranged and forced marriages. If we were normal, you two would both be married off by the time you were twelve years old."

"Is that why we are running away, Roya?" Shafika, the practical one, questions.

"You know about that?" I ask, surprised.

"We overhear things, Roya," admits Nooria. "I'm ready to go. This village has nothing for us. Hopefully Father will find us wherever we go. I really hope it will be better than here."

"We will be on a dangerous adventure," Monisa points out. "But I believe there are kinder, more female-friendly, no, more female-respectful, corners of the world for us to live in."

Mother returns at that moment. "Hi girls. Roya, how is Ghulam?"

"Aunt Fahima, Mother sent us with soup for Ghulam," Nooria happily interjects.

"How is he?" Mother asks again.

"He is the same, Mother. He still hasn't regained consciousness."

"Well, I guess more prayers are needed. Girls, thank your mother for the soup. Shall we all have a little tea and then say our evening prayers?"

We all nod and look at one another. Later I will tell Mother my cousins know of the plan. Right now, we need to check on Ghulam again and go to evening prayers.

Chapter 18:
FAHIMA—A PRAYER TO ALLAH

Allah, this is your obedient servant Fahima praising You above all others for the many blessings you have bestowed on my family and me. Today I seek Your guidance on this very difficult and dangerous journey I must take to save Your subjects here in this small village from the violence and corruption that is being waged in Your name.

Please Almighty One, please show me what is the best thing to do to move those around me to a place where we can better serve you. We give You all praise and worship. I humbly acknowledge the things You have done for me all my life, and with great reluctance ask You to bless me again so that I may lead our small group from this place to a better place in Your kingdom where You are more respected and obeyed.

I know that I am but a humble woman, but believe in Your infinite wisdom that You have placed women on this earth to serve You and to be a help maid to our men. I have tried to do that, but the response from the men around me has not been what I believe you ordained. That is not true about my husband nor the men in my family, as you know. But the men who make up our village and surrounding villages, all the way up to our country's leaders, do not seem to recognize women's part in Your supreme plan. I believe You have blessed me by sending Ghulam back to me as a chaperone and protector on our travels.

Almighty One, I implore You to guide my mind and hand and enable me to lead this small group of Your servants out of this wilderness of disrespect and violence into another, better place. I have spent my whole life trying to follow Your direction, and hope that this last attempt at survival pleases You and is in Your plan for my life and the others who journey with me.

Please accept my good friend Jahan into Your heavenly kingdom and allow her to also watch over my brood of journeyers and me. Please keep Mother Uzra and Rahmat safe when we cannot be together.

I am Your humble servant. All is blessed in Your name.

Chapter 19:
UZRA—WORD IS SPREADING

"Mullah Aman, may Allah be with you this morning."

"And you, Uzra Abulzir. I see you are alone today. Has your daughter-in law Fahima and granddaughter Roya left you? And how is your grandson Ghulam healing? Has he returned to Kashar's militia yet?"

"Ah, Aman, it is kind that you keep such notice of my family. As I age, I seem to have less and less energy to stay abreast of their activities."

"Indeed, Uzra. We are both getting older, as is Allah's wish. It has been many years since we were in school together."

"Those days are very far memories now, Aman."

"You and your husband did well raising your sons Rahmat and Mahmoud. It is sad that your husband left you so many years alone."

"Praise to Allah I had him the years I did. You will remember that he was a good father and husband."

"Yes, Uzra I do remember. He was a good man. This village misses him. I miss him."

I smile and nod in agreement. My husband and Aman were friends in school. Both worked to keep the village safe and progressing. Aman did not approve of us sending Mahmoud and Rahmat to Kabul for advanced learning, however. He has always brought that up, and even after all these years still seems to have some resentment. I think he believes their educations somehow diminish his authority. Well, it cannot be helped. We wanted more for our children than just this village.

"So, Uzra, where are your daughter-in-law and grandchildren?"

"Ah, they have traveled out to Omar and Hawa's farm to gather some necessary supplies for the trip to Quandahar. Roya is escorting some of the children for their vaccinations and Fahima and Ghulam are going along to get some needed medical attention for Ghulam."

"I see," says Mullah Aman, looking around the room for signs of something out of the ordinary. "I should have sent them with a blessing," he eventually murmurs, finding nothing out of order. "I have done so for other families leaving for Quandahar."

"We are so sorry we didn't think of that before they left. They wanted to get to Hawa's early, hoping not to run into Walizada and his men."

"I can understand that. Walizada is unpredictable and with children with them Fahima and Roya must be careful. I assume Ghulam is healthy enough to chaperone them?"

"He is doing much better after the herbs that Jahan provided just before she died. She was such a blessing and is in Allah's hands now."

"Well," the little man says stroking his beard as he forms his parting thought, "may Allah bless and protect them on their journey and bring them back safely to you and the other children's families."

"Thank you, Mullah Aman. We are blessed to have your wisdom and kindness in our village. May Allah bless and keep you, also."

"Good day, Uzra."

"Good day, Mullah Aman."

Part 11:
THE JOURNEY BEGINS

Chapter 20:
HAWA—SACRIFICES

Omar and Hawa's Farm Outside Dand

"Omar, I see Fahima and her party coming up the road. Open the shed doors so they can drive in. Walizada will be here today for more poppies, and he must not see Fahima and her truckload of children."

"Yes, Mother." Young Omar dashes off to a broken-down shed and props the doors open so the truck Fahima is arriving in can drive inside.

If Walizada sees Fahima and her band of children, he will stop it and use Fahima as a bargaining chip with Kashar. He could also figure out what Fahima is planning to do and destroy all her plans. Those children would be doomed to the madrassa and Fahima, Roya, and the rest of the women used by Walizada in his drug trade.

"Mother, I hear the truck approaching. The shed is open and the supplies you have gathered for them are ready to load in the truck. Pooch is sitting next to the bag of rice. He believes he is going on this journey. That crafty dog," Omar says.

"I'm not sure who is crazier, Pooch or Fahima, to want to go on this journey. But they need our help or it will not happen."

"I think Fahima and Roya are very brave to want to save the children, Mother."

"Ah, Omar my youngest. You read too many fairy books. What Fahima is about to do is very, very dangerous, and she could end up getting them all killed. The Taliban, Kashar, and Walizada will all be out to defeat her once they realize what has happened. They will make her and her band of rebellious women pay for disobeying their rules if they are caught, by any of them. Women are pawns in the war games these men play. Fahima has seen through that and is desperately trying to get out from under their abusive expectations."

"Is that why you have agreed to help them?"

"Yes, and I want to see just a few young boys stay out of the clutches of the Mullahs and their violent brainwashing. I guess I feel a little guilty because your father and I were able to keep you and your brothers out of the madrassa and here on the farm with us. But that too, had a price, because in order to do that we have to grow the poppies for Walizada's drugs. It is not noble, but we have survived. Fahima's quest is noble, and I want to play a small part in it. Now go, help Ghulam guide the truck in and load it quickly so they can be out of here before Walizada comes."

"Yes, Mother."

An ancient truck rumbles down the dirt road to the farm, a cloud of dust shrouding the canvas top and the band of women and small children huddled inside. The tires are almost bald and occasionally it backfires a puff of black smoke. The windshield is cracked, and Ghulam labors to shift gears. Fahima is next to him in the cab, directing him to Hawa's farm. As they approach, Omar waves them toward the open shed doors. Ghulam acknowledges and soon has the truck inside the shed.

"Ghulam, couldn't you find a quieter truck?" I laugh.

"Hawa, you know these days most large vehicles are confiscated by Kashar for militia use. This one was dead and Moommar resurrected it for us."

"Are you a good mechanic?"

"No, not really. I can figure things out given enough time, but on this mission we may not have time."

"Mother, I could go along to help. You know I am a good mechanic. Besides having two adult males to chaperone these women and children is better than just one. What if something happened to Ghulam?"

"Omar, you are only fifteen years old. You have not seen the world."

"Hawa, I do not mean to be disrespectful, but I was only fifteen when I went to the militia with my father," Ghulam softly notes.

Hawa looks to Fahima, now standing next to Ghulam. "Fahima, do you want to honor my Omar's request and allow him to travel with you? He is another mouth to feed but is good at keeping vehicles running. Omar is who his father turns to when vehicles here need work. Ghulam is injured and driving this old truck could be too much for him. Omar is a good driver, as well as a mechanic."

"Hawa, you know how dangerous this trip is for us. Are you willing to let your youngest son leave the safety of your farm to join us?"

"The safety here at the farm is not guaranteed. At any time Walizada, the Taliban, or the militia could decide they have had enough of us and destroy us. I would feel better if Omar were with you. I would say that with Omar you are going to get Pooch, too. Pooch will not let Omar go without following him, so you might as well include him. Pooch is good at catching rabbits and sniffing out landmines. He could prove more valuable than Omar. Pooch loves children. He will be another pair of eyes to keep them safe."

Fahima smiles at my remarks and understands the magnitude of the decision I have just made—sending my youngest son with her into the unknown.

"As always, Hawa, you are generous and wise. I will do my very best to keep both Omar and Pooch safe."

"Okay, then, let's get this truck loaded and out of here before Walizada and his band of thugs come for their drugs."

Roya, Monisa, Nooria, and Shafika jump out of the back of the truck to help load. Noor and the other little boys jump out to pet Pooch, while Sakina, Maky, and Fawigia organize the loaded supplies. Yasmine sits quietly on the bench. Her missing leg makes it hard to get in and out of the truck, so she waits.

Thirty minutes later, all is loaded, the children are back in the back of the truck, and Fahima and I stand going through our mental checklists, silently making sure everything has been considered.

"Well Hawa, it is time," Fahima turns to me and grabs my rough hand. "Without you and your generosity, this adventure would never have gotten started. We owe much to you and your husband."

"Fahima, as mothers and women Allah has expected us to do the best for the children He has blessed us with. You and Roya and the rest of your troop have taken that beyond your own children and embraced others. Every day I will pray that you are all safe and that you find the peace and respect you are searching for. I may join you should my responsibilities here change. Right now Allah has chosen me to be here, but know that my heart is with you and the others in seeking something better both for our children and ourselves. I send my youngest with you in hopes that you can do what I cannot. May Allah bless you."

Fahima and I both wipe tears from our cheeks, embrace, and, without another word, Fahima jumps in the cab of the truck with Ghulam and Omar and the truck backs out of the shed and begins to drive up the road. *I love you, Omar. Please, Allah, see that he is safe since I cannot.* I turn and close the shed doors and walk back to my world.

Chapter 21:
FAHIMA—FIRST NIGHT

Riverbank, on the Road to Qandahar

"Ghulam, how much longer to Qandahar? I know the children and women riding in the back must be exhausted. We should stop soon."

"Mother," Ghulam struggles to steer around the pocks in the road, fearing that if he swerves too much it might land them on an IED or landmine. "It is very slow going with this old truck. We may not make it until deep into the night."

"We have to consider the children. Would it be safe to camp for the night somewhere off the road?"

"The militia has been through here many times. We might be able to rest at Darweshan along the river. I know of a place if there is no one there right now."

"We have three days to get to the vaccination clinic in Qandahar, so we do have time."

"Fahima," Omar joins the conversation, "camping by the river gives us a little protection. If we are attacked, at least they cannot come from the river side."

"Yes," says Ghulam, "But then we have no escape route."

"Boys, if we are attacked there is no escaping anyhow. We cannot outrun anyone—Taliban, militia, or Walizada and his drug gang."

"That is true, Mother. If we are discovered, there is not much chance of escape. The river is high right now and getting across it would be difficult with the vehicles they use, so it is unlikely they will be running along it."

"I am not a military strategist, but I know women and children and we must stop soon. The first night will be the most difficult to get settled and figure out food, sleeping, bathing, and so on."

Ghulam laughs. "Mother you are not exactly the outdoor type. Have you ever slept under the stars?"

I have to chuckle at his statement. "Well, no. But I have had to live in some very primitive places lately and sleeping under the stars might be an improvement from those places."

"We might need some of Omar's family's Bedouin ways to get us through this adventure." Ghulam smiles and turns to wink at Omar.

"Sure. Some of my mother's people still live that way. When I was smaller, we used to visit my grandparents and there was one old uncle who still lived in a tent with his crazy camel."

"Crazy camel," remarks Ghulam, "That is a good name for this wreck of a truck: the Crazy Camel."

"I have to say, since we have left our village hoping for it to be for good, we are becoming Bedouins and I guess this vehicle is like our camel. If only it could go without gas like camels can go without water."

Both young men laugh out loud.

Within ten miles, Ghulam turns off the highway and we head for the river. It has been a couple of hours since we last stopped, so I'm sure our passengers are ready to get out and stretch their legs. And I would bet the little boys are hungry.

"Is it far, Ghulam?"

"There is a crossroads at the river, and I am thinking that we can take the back road into Qandahar. Since we are going to the vaccination clinic like everyone else, we are not yet fugitives. We are less likely to encounter any troops, but if we encounter patrols, we do have reason to be out on the roads."

"Good thinking, Ghulam. So far our adventure is blessed by Mullah Aman."

"Over there, Ghulam," Omar points to a stand of trees about fifty yards from the rapidly flowing river.

"I see it too, Omar," Ghulam nods and begins to turn the steering wheel to slowly maneuver the truck into the trees. He parks with the hood pointed toward the river and turns the engine off.

In an instant there are laughing, running voices as the little boys are the first out of the truck with one shaggy dog running behind them. I hop out to survey things and check on the women.

"Cousin Fahima, it is really peaceful here," says Monisa as she stretches her back. She helps Maky out of the truck. Maky has little Jalil on her hip. He is too small to hop down and is only just beginning to walk, so the uneven ground is too difficult.

"Thank you, Monisa." Maky gets down out of the truck and immediately looks for Noor. "Noor, not too close to the river. That swift-moving water will take you under in the blink of an eye."

Noor waves back and changes his direction to parallel the river with Hakim and Wakil, Yasmine's little brothers, right behind him. Struggling to keep up behind them is little Laila, Yasmine's baby sister, determined to be with the boys.

Sakina looks on and says, "Roya, I can see how your job as teacher is a difficult one. I am not used to rowdy little boys. My girls were always calmer."

"Really, Mother," says Shafika, "Nooria was calm, but I have always been freer."

"That is true." Sakina puts her arm around Nooria's shoulders, "But you have always been the responsible, serious one." Nooria smiles and Shafika dashes off to follow the little boys.

"Boys are a challenge with their boundless energy," replies Roya, "But Shafika is right. Girls can be just as challenging."

Fawigia helps Yasmine out of the back of the truck. Her mother holds Yasmine's prosthetic leg until she is on the ground, then helps her attach it.

"Well, you don't have to worry about me anymore, Miss Roya," Yasmine says as she adjusts her false leg under her print skirt. "I'm with Nooria, now." Nooria responds with a pained look on her face. For no apparent reason, Nooria feels responsible for Yasmine, and I am quite sure will be helping her in every way she can on this journey. Nooria is just like that.

Omar starts a fire and Sakina, Fawigia, and I sort through our supplies to fashion a meal. It is light quite long this time of year, so once the sun goes down the children should be ready to sleep.

Ghulam pokes the fire, "Mother, Omar and I will see that the fire is burning all night so the children stay warm and any animals around will stay away."

"Thank you, darling." The children find their spots around the fire and roll up in prayer rugs to sleep. Within minutes there are little snores. *So far so good*, I think. *It surely won't be this easy the whole time. Many thanks, Allah, for today.*

Chapter 22:
ROYA—DIRECTION?

I hand Mother a hot cup of tea and sit down next to her around the fire. Sakina, Maky, and Fawigia are busy calming the children to sleep and Ghulam and Omar are checking out the truck after the day's miles. Pooch is right by Omar's side.

"Mother, we have done it. Begun our escape. Do you know where we will go after Qandahar?"

"Roya, I have a vague notion, but events as they unroll will dictate how we proceed from the vaccination clinic. Staying with Cousin Basra is reasonable, but everyone will be expecting us to return home quickly to get the children back in school. Since you are their teacher, it is doubly obvious that returning home is crucial. We can maybe gain a day or two with the explanation that Ghulam needs to see a doctor, but even that only buys us a few days."

"Well, the break for vaccinations is a week, so we do have a little time."

"Yes, darling, but to avoid suspicion we need to leave with everyone else. I believe we need to head north of Kabul, avoiding Kabul at all costs, and head into the mountains. Living in the mountains is a hard life, but affords us more places to hide."

"You don't mean into Khyber Pass, do you? I understand that is very dangerous. The Taliban and the drug dealers pass through there going back and forth from Pakistan."

"No, we will avoid Khyber Pass and head the other way. Ghulam has said that generally the Taliban moves through the Pass to Kabul and then spreads out to Helmand and Herat provinces."

"There are no guarantees, though, are there?"

"No, Roya, this whole escape is a deadly gamble. I feel so guilty exposing Aunt Sakina and Maky and Fawigia and their children to such danger, but in my heart know this is the best way."

"I'm sure Allah will help us."

"We must all pray that He does."

As we are sipping our tea, Fawigia comes and sits next to us. "Fahima, I overheard your conversation with Roya and I have something I would like to add."

"Of course, Fawigia," Mother says. "We are all in this together."

"You may not know that my people are Hazara. I have extended family within 100 kilometers of Bamyan. As you probably know, that is a Buddhist colony. The Taliban has already been through there and destroyed the enormous sacred Buddhist statues and religious artifacts. Once they did that, they did not come back. They did what they intended to and left it in rubble."

"Fawigia, I have read about the Buddhist religion. Their culture and beliefs do seem to be gentler and kinder than where we are right now in our ways of Islam."

"Fahima, I think that would be a good place for us to start over. With their kind help, we may be able to find a safe haven for ourselves and our children."

Mother contemplates for a minute Fawigia's remarks and then says, "I agree. It is good to know that if we go to the Bamiyan Valley that we will have family there. Fawigia, when is the last time you saw your family?"

"It has been a while, of course. Understand that my family follows Islam, but since they have lived alongside the Buddhists all these years, they are knowledgeable and sympathetic to their way of life."

"Roya, did you study or read about the Buddhists?"

"A little Mother, I do know some of their basic beliefs. I think Fawigia is right. It might be a good place if we want to stay in our own country, to begin a better way of life."

We are all silent for a moment, then Mother says, "That is the real decision, isn't it? Do we leave our country and seek a better life in a foreign country, or do we stay and try to plant the seeds of change in our own. All we know is Afghanistan," whispers Fawigia. "It is in our blood. Our ancestors have fought many invaders over the centuries and given their lives for the life we have today. Somewhere along the way, we have turned on ourselves. Our men our determined to battle one another for their inflated beliefs. Can we women help them see that we are our own enemies? Too many years of fighting have destroyed families and created a culture of violence. I do not want my sons and my daughters to follow that depravity."

Mother puts her arm around Fawigia's shoulder and softly says in her ear, "That is our mission."

"Let us pray to Allah," Mother says, "and seek His wisdom and grace for our actions."

"Let's," I say. As the fire burns on, we say our prayers and then join the little bundles of sleeping children for the night.

Chapter 23:
ROYA—MY CLEVER STUDENT

"Good morning, Mother. Were you able to sleep? Are you ready for your tea?"

"Thank you, Roya. Last night was a little hard, I am not used to sleeping under the stars as Ghulam says. I was nervous and uncomfortable."

"Me, too. In my classroom I have more boundaries to round up my students. Out here, they have more room to wander, and it requires more energy to keep up with them. There are also more dangers."

"Indeed, Roya. We must pray that Allah keeps all of us in His sights."

"Look Mother, Noor has gone to help Ghulam and Omar. Poor little guy is probably happy to see men, even if they are young men, since it has been so long since he has seen his father and there are so few healthy, regular men in the village."

Stepping up on the running board of the truck, Noor hangs on to the rearview mirror and tries to look into the truck engine where Ghulam and Omar are working.

"Hey, guys, what are you doing?" the little guy asks with a big smile on his face.

"We are making sure the fluid levels are good," says Omar.

"Oh," says Noor with a crease developing in his brown forehead. "I bet that is important."

"Very important," grins Ghulam, then grabs him by the waist and holds him so he can see directly into the truck engine. "There, can you see better?"

"Yes, but I am big enough to do it myself." Ghulam lets him find his footing on the bumper and lean under the hood to watch Omar check the oil level. "How did you learn about trucks, Omar?" he asks.

"My father and my older brothers showed me. On the farm you must figure things out when they break down, so that's how I learned." Omar puts the oil stick back after checking the level and wiping it clean.

"Omar is good at this, Noor," says Ghulam. "I have not been around trucks, so my knowledge is not so good."

"You mean there are things you do not learn in school?" Noor questions.

Ghulam laughs, "Yes, Noor, we cannot learn everything about life in school. But that is not to say one shouldn't go to school and learn all they can there. My sister, Roya, is a good teacher, don't you think?"

"Oh yes, I love Miss Roya, but did not know you could learn things outside of school. Omar, Ghulam, did you go to the madrassa or to Miss Roya's school?"

"I went to Miss Roya's school," adds Omar. "I was not forced to the madrassa, so I have learned much from being on the farm. I like to read also, and one learns a lot from books."

"I actually went to higher school in Kabul, Noor," says Ghulam. "I have also learned a lot from books. I, too, was not forced to go to the madrassa. When I was growing up, the mujahadeens and the madrassas did not exist. The Taliban has brought that to our villages."

"Mullah Aman wants me to go to the madrassa," comments Noor. "I want to stay with Miss Roya, although I think it would be great to go to school with all boys and not have to put up with the girls like Shafika and Yasmine. I like Nooria since her name is like mine and she is older."

Ghulam and Omar laugh. "Believe me, little buddy, girls will be more important in your life as you get older," says Ghulam with a sage look on his face.

"I don't know, Noor," says Omar "I have been on the farm so long I don't even know any girls. I will have to let you know about that."

"I do know it is our duty as men to protect the girls, right Ghulam?" Noor gets a serious look on his face as he questions Ghulam.

"That is correct, Noor. In our culture men are the providers and protectors," Ghulam takes Noor around the waist again and sets him down on the ground. "But for right now you must obey your mother, right?"

"I got it. But I will protect her too." Noor turns and runs off to find some breakfast.

Ghulam turns back to Omar, "That little guy is very sharp. I can see why Mother and Roya and his mother want to keep him out of the madrassa."

"I understand, too. I also understand that it is our duty as the men of this party to protect them all. This is new for me. My father and brothers were always there to protect my mother. We have no other girls and Mother is pretty capable of protecting herself."

"I don't know your mother well, but she sure does appear to be able to take care of herself. My mother is educated and smart but has not had a lot of experience protecting herself. We have a big duty to make sure this group of women, girls, and little boys get where we are going safely."

Omar scratches his head and says, "Well, this journey should teach me a lot about girls. There are more here than I have ever been around at one time."

Ghulam laughs, "Get ready, they can be a challenge. Take it from one that grew up with a big sister. Now let's find some breakfast so we can hit the road."

Ghulam and Omar walk back toward the fire and circle of women with hungry looks on their faces.

Chapter 24:
KASHAR—DANGEROUS LIAISONS

Militia Encampment, Two Days after Escape Launch

"Zalmai, what news do you bring from Mullah Aman?" Kashar finishes trimming his meticulously groomed white beard in the rear mirror of a transport vehicle and turns to address his son.

"Kashar, Father—Mullah Aman reports that the women and children have left the village for Qandahar for their annual inoculations. Ghulam is escorting his mother and sister, the village teacher, with seven or eight of the children and their mothers. It looks like Ghulam has recovered from his wounds enough to drive a truck."

Kashar sheaths the razor and turns to look into the face that reminds him every day of his departed wife. "Sending Ghulam home to heal from his wounds has accomplished another thing—he can accompany the women and children and I don't have to send a fighter. Good. And we don't have to use one of our trucks for such a purpose. Are there any reports of Taliban in Qandahar?"

"According to our sources, the Taliban has focused elsewhere because it is the week of children coming in for shots. The United Nations' troops are there to see that everything goes well, so we can also focus on other parts of the area. Do you agree, Father?"

"We have seen this before. There is a brief truce with the Taliban to allow the children to be cared for. We have all seen the terrible diseases and suffering that happens when these small ones are not properly protected from illnesses. It is a protection we cannot give them with our guns and explosives."

"What do we do in the meantime, Father?" Zalmai walks with Kashar to the building fifty yards from the parked vehicle and they enter a room covered with maps and neatly stacked guns.

Kashar walks to a desk and picks up a calendar. "It is true we have a short rest from worrying about the village women and children, but our next concern should be the whereabouts of Walizada. It is just about time for the poppies to be harvested, and he will be down from the hills to pick up his evil product."

"Why do we not stop him, Father?" Zalmai asks.

"Because he funds us just enough to keep the Taliban off his back, son." Kashar sits at his desk with a deep sigh. "Right now, he is half ally and half enemy. It would be best if he joined us in protecting and defending our homeland and people, but the taste of heroin and the money and power it gives him makes him less interested in the good fight and more invested in his drug trade and life secure in the mountains away from the real fighting."

"And the truth is Father, half of our men seek his heroin. Without that taste of decadence, they might leave us and join him." Zalmai sits in front of the desk, picks up a rifle, and begins cleaning the dust and grime from it.

"Son, there is too much truth in what you say. It is a confusing holy war we fight here trying to protect our villages from the invading religious zealots of the Taliban and our own infidel countrymen, cousins, and neighbors spilling drugs and violence through our homeland."

"What keeps you going, Father?" Zalmai looks up from his work to see his father rubbing his beard and staring out the doorway with a determined look.

"At first it was my religious beliefs. I believed Allah had willed that we take up arms against the unholy invaders. Much of it was to avenge your mother's death at the hands of the Taliban. Most of it was to protect you and your brother. I find myself stuck between two violent factions of our own people, in a cycle of fighting I can't get out of, son."

"All I can remember is fighting. I can't imagine, Father, what life would be without it. I don't know what normal is." Zalmai searches his father's weathered face for a response.

"I know, Son. When I started this fight, I believed it was to provide a world where you and your brother could live and prosper. I was enraged that they took your mother from you. I wanted to right that wrong and set the world straight again. That goal seems further and further away each year that passes."

"Father, Ahmad and I are devoted to serving with you in whatever you direct us to do. Wives, homes, families are not Allah's wish for us."

"Zalmai, that is not true. Allah wishes for all of us to live peaceful, devout lives. Without your mother that is lost to me. I fear I have made it lost to you and your brother as well."

"Without you, Father, and the resistance we provide, Allah's will could never be accomplished. We are not there yet, but I believe you will get us there. We will defeat our own infidels and re-find the village life Allah intended."

Kashar stands and walks to the other side of the desk and puts an arm around the shoulders of his oldest son and says, "Inshallah." He walks back to the desk, looks at the calendar, and looks up again at

Zalmai. "Zalmai put together about twenty fighters. We need to go to Omar's farm and ensure that when Walizada comes for his poppies he only takes what is due him and leaves Omar and his family well. Also, have Rahmat go with the group to take care of the money Walizada owes us."

"Yes, Father."

Chapter 25:
FAHIMA—THE AGREEMENT

River Camp Site, Day Two

Fahima finishes her morning prayers and returns to the fire to help Sakina, Maky, Fawigia, Roya, and Monisa feed the children and break camp for the journey on to Qandahar.

"Good morning, ladies," Fahima takes her prayer rug, puts it in the back of the truck, and walks to the fire to pour a cup of tea.

Fawigia offers her a small dollop of honey then asks, "Fahima, what happens after Qandahar?"

Fahima sips her tea then replies, "Right now I think we should leave before the week of immunizations is over, so we are moving on the road with the rest of the groups of children going back to their villages. We will be less suspicious."

"Of course. I will try to contact my people in Hazara while we are in Qandahar to let them know we are coming."

"That would be good, Fawigia."

"Fahima, while we are in Qandahar will I be able to contact Mahmoud to let him know our plan?" Sakina searches Fahima's eyes for her answer.

"Ah, sister, I think we had better keep our ultimate destination to ourselves for now. If Mahmoud knows anything, we could put him in danger. You can tell him we are leaving Qandahar, but please do not tell him where we are headed. We might not end up there anyhow. The less he knows the safer he will be."

"Fahima, Mahmoud does not care about his safety."

"I know, but the fewer people who know where we are going, the better chance we have to make it."

"You are probably right, but I never keep things from him."

"I know. I know this whole ordeal is going against all our instincts but one—to save the children."

Monisa puts little Lalia down and walks over to Fahima, Fawigia, and Sakina. "Cousin Fahima, we are doing much more than saving the children. We are saving ourselves from the indignities of our own culture. We can't save the children if we can't save ourselves."

She touches Monisa's cheek and searches her eyes, "Monisa you are right. This escape, if that's what we call it, is for all of us."

"Mother, Monisa and I, and probably Maky, only know women's treatment as it is today. You have seen another way, however briefly. You hold the vision of what freedom for women can be in this country." Roya picks up Maky's Jalil and wipes his face as she moves toward the fire.

"It is true I have tasted a freedom you young women have not. And yes, I seek that for all of us, but especially you young ones. To me, you are these small children with your future clouded by restrictions and lack of respect. You are all my children."

"But we are not children, Fahima," Fawigia says. "Some of us are mothers with our own children. My Yasmine is lame because of the fighting. Maky's Noor was bound for the madrassa. Sakina's Shafika and Nooria were destined to a life like Roya and Monisa. This escape is about all of us."

"I wanted to keep it simple," Fahima admits. "But you are right. Underlying all my concern for Noor and the madrassa is a deeper concern for all of the females."

"Mother, you cannot fight this alone," Roya reminds her. "We are all part of this."

"Yes, that is true. But I want you all to promise that if we get caught and are apprehended for our disobedience that you will all admit that I am the leader and the one to blame. Please let me take the blame and the consequences for it all."

"We cannot let you do that, Cousin," Monisa says.

"Of course not," Fawigia and Sakina nod in agreement.

"No," insists Fahima, "I have to take the blame and the consequences of our actions. Because you all must carry on even if something happens to me."

"Agreed," Sakina, Maky, and Fawigia say in unison.

"Not sure I agree," says Monisa. "But we will carry on as best we can if something happens to you."

"Mother, you have started this. We will continue and take it as far as we can and hope that the children, when they mature, will also carry on. Shafika, Nooria, Yasmine, and little Laila and all the boys need a better future. Ghulam and Omar and all his brothers, too." Roya smiles and puts her arm around her brother as he and Omar walk up to the fire.

"Time to hit the road, ladies." Ghulam begins to extinguish the fire. "Let's pack up and move on."

Chapter 26:
RAHMAT—FAHIMA'S QUEST

Omar and Hawa's Farm, Day 2

"Kashar, you wish for me to give Walizada the list of weapons you seek and the cost?"

"Rahmat, Walizada knows what we need, and he knows what it costs," Kashar gazes out the window of the truck and seems to be calculating other things in his head. "I count on you to make the most of our meeting and to get as much money as you can from him. He knows that without the militia his drug business would not be as successful."

"Do I negotiate the drugs we will need for our own men?" I know Kashar does not like to acknowledge that the men of the militia indulge in such undisciplined behavior, but we all know some will only fight if they receive their highs.

"No," Kashar turns his attention back to me and says, "We will let Raz do that. He seems to have a better relationship with Walizada since he once worked for him. I want you to get the money Walizada owes us and be done. Do you understand?"

"Yes, Kashar. I know my job." The truck rolls into the farm of Omar and Hawa and stops in front of their house. Walizada has not yet arrived. He likes to keep Kashar waiting to make himself seem more important. Kashar tolerates the disrespect only because he needs Walizada's dirty money to fund the militia. Omar limps out to greet

Kashar. His crutch thuds as he walks across the hard-packed dirt to greet Kashar. Hawa is at his side, as always since he lost his lower left leg to a landmine. Kashar normally does not tolerate women around when talking weapons and money, but he tolerates Hawa since it was one of his IEDs that Omar stepped on and lost his leg.

"Kashar, welcome. Good to see you." Omar makes his way to the side of the truck and shakes hands with Kashar through the truck window. "Rahmat, Inshallah."

"Omar, my friend," Kashar turns his attention to Omar and quickly eyes Hawa then focuses back on Omar. "Is our friend Walizada here yet?"

"No, Kashar. The poppies are ready. I think he can smell when they are to be harvested and comes down from the mountains like the sheep in spring."

Kashar pulls on his white beard and smiles. "Omar, I can always count on you for an interesting comment on the day."

Omar smiles and steps back so Kashar can get out of the truck. Kashar looks at Hawa and says, "Hawa, Inshallah. May I speak with your husband alone? You can tell Rahmat of his family while I talk business with Omar. I'm sure the business talk will bore you, and Rahmat is anxious to hear of his family. Have you seen or know of Ghulam and how his wound is doing?"

Hawa steps back from Omar and with a devilish grin says, "Kashar, I do not often get to the village these days but have seen Fahima and do have news for Rahmat."

"Hawa," I say as I get out of the back of the truck, "May I have a cup of tea and hear your news of my family?"

"Rahmat, please come in and I will tell you of my last talk with Fahima. I have not seen Ghulam but do know his mother seemed hopeful he is recovering well. Come. Let's have tea. Kashar, would you like tea also?"

"No, Hawa. Omar and I will talk and then Walizada will be here. Please, take Rahmat with you."

Hawa and I turn and walk to the door of the house in silence. Inside I sit while Hawa makes tea.

"Rahmat, are we out of hearing of Kashar?" Hawa's expression turns serious.

"Kashar reads people like a book, but his hearing is not the best given the many years he has been around guns and explosives.

"Good, because I have important news that must not get to him." Hawa pours water into a kettle for the tea.

"How is my family?"

"Rahmat, they have left Dand and are heading north." Hawa lights the stove and then sits across from me. "She has done it."

"Done what, Hawa?"

"She has taken a small band of children and women and plans to find a better place for them."

"What do you mean, Hawa?"

"Rahmat, your Fahima has followed her heart and is trying to take Roya and Ghulam, Sakina and her girls, and a few others from the village to start over in a place where women and children are better treated."

"Hawa, I know my Fahima is an idealist and was crushed when the days of freedom and education for women were taken away by the Taliban, but to defy all and think she can start her own village is crazy."

"Crazy or not she is doing it. She is on her way to Qandahar to have the children vaccinated and does not plan to return to Dand."

"Where does she plan to go? How does she plan to survive? Both my children are with her?"

"Ghulam has recovered enough to drive an old truck they found and revived. My little Omar is also with them to help keep the truck running and to act as an additional male escort."

Hawa pours the boiling water in the cups and the tea begins to brew.

"This news will certainly change my prayers. I was always fearful for Fahima and Roya's safety in the village, but now, on the road, moving to another place. I am not sure I can withstand the worry."

"Rahmat," Hawa looks at me with intensity and says, "She believes this is Allah's will. I think she is right. It takes someone brave and clever and strong to do something like this, and she is all of those things."

"Yes, she is," I must agree with Hawa. "Fahima has always been far smarter and braver than most men I know. This is going to be difficult and dangerous. Being with Kashar and the militia I was aware of goings on in the village and had some ability to play a part in protecting them. Now, they are out of my realm. Heading north, I have no ability to do anything for them. They are truly on their own."

"Well, Rahmat, they do have Allah leading the way." She smiles and sips her cooling tea.

"I hope you are correct, Hawa. Fahima without Allah's help could be in for defeat."

"This is not a win and conquer attempt, Rahmat. We are women. We really don't think like that. This is a move to protect the children. Little Noor was to go to the madrassa and that is what lit the fire in Fahima. She couldn't stand to see one more child go through that violent indoctrination."

"I suppose you are right. As always, Fahima's actions are for the children. Ultimately, she is working to create a better world for her own grown children. Both Roya and Ghulam are yet to start their families. I can see Fahima building a better world for her grandchildren."

"And build she will, Rahmat."

"Hawa, I must go. Many thanks for the news and for the help and support you have given my family. I will use you as a communication point if Fahima is able to get word to you. I can't protect her on her quest, but maybe I can find some money to help feed and fund her journey."

"I will be happy to do what I can. My son is part of this journey as well."

"Of course, Hawa. We both have much invested in Fahima's success."

"Inshallah, Rahmat," Hawa bear hugs me, and I turn and walk out to join Kashar and Omar who are watching Walizada and his men pull in the yard.

Chapter 27:
FAHIMA—GIRLS UNDER SIEGE

Qandahar, Day 3

"Cousin Basra, it is so kind of you to open your home to all of us while we have the children here in Qandahar. I remember the many years we used to visit as children. Your mother and my mother sipping tea while we girls hid away to talk." Cousin Basra smiles and begins to lead us in from the street.

"Oh Fahima, it has been many years. We have worried about you and Rahmat, so far away in your little village. It is so good to see that you are well. How is Rahmat?" Basra left the village many years ago when she married Hassan. Her home is as I remember it, quiet and warm with the wonderful smells of the market just up the street.

"Roya, Monisa, please say hello to Cousin Basra," both Roya and Monisa shake the road dust from their clothes and walk up next to me.

"Cousin Basra," says Roya, "Mother has spoken so much of you. It is so nice to finally meet someone from the family and Mother's past." Roya hugs Basra.

"Nice of you to have us," Monisa adds.

"Fahima," says Basra standing back from Roya's hug and looking her up and down. "This beautiful daughter of yours has Rahmat's eyes and your sweet mouth. I'm guessing she probably is as smart as you both. You and Rahmat were always so good in school and the university."

"Basra, this is also our son, Ghulam." Ghulam limps up after parking the truck near Basra's door to the street.

"Oh my, Fahima. So handsome," Basra turns and smiles at Ghulam. "And who are the rest of your traveling party?"

"Of course, the rest of your guests." The back of the truck continues to empty. Maky steps down with Jalil in her arms and Noor at her side.

"Basra, this is a neighbor from Dand, Maky and her two sons, little Jalil and Noor. Noor is one of Roya's students."

"Ah," says Basra stepping up to pat little Jalil on the cheek and look down at Noor. "Welcome Maky, Inshallah."

"Thank you, Madame Basra," says Maky. "It is so kind of you to host us while we are in Qandahar."

"Our pleasure. It has been a while since I have seen such beautiful children. I understand your husband is here in Qandahar working."

"He is," reassures Maky. "I hope you won't mind us reuniting in your home while we are here."

"Of course not, dear. It must be hard to be apart and you by yourself raising the children while he works so far away."

"Good neighbors like Fahima make it a little easier." Maky smiles and looks over at me.

"Basra," I move Maky and the boys on and bring up the rest of the passengers from the truck to meet Basra. "Here we have my sister-in-law Sakina and her two daughters, Shafika and Nooria. Rahmat's brother Mahmoud is also here in Qandahar working."

Sakina gently pushes the two somewhat reluctant girls forward to meet Basra. "Madame Basra, it is such a pleasure to meet you. This is Nooria, my oldest, and Shafika, our youngest. Girls …"

"Inshallah, Madame Basra," says Nooria shyly.

Shafika takes a step forward, smiles at Basra, and says, "Inshallah, Madame Basra. It must be so wonderful to live just up the street from the market." She eyes the marketplace up the street over Basra's shoulder.

"Shafika," warns Sakina. "Be polite."

Basra laughs. "Yes, it is convenient, but it can be a temptation for young girls from the villages." She throws a knowing look to Fahima and back to Sakina.

"Basra, let me introduce you to the rest of our little band of travelers. This is Fawigia and her children Little Laila, Hakim, Wakil, and Yasmine."

"Fawigia, it is a pleasure to have you and your lovely children in my home," Basra looks all the children over and then steps up to Yasmine. "I see this lovely one with such a head of beautiful hair has met with misfortune." She has noticed Yasmine's artificial leg and her difficulty walking on the uneven street.

"Madame Basra," says Fawigia, "We are so honored to be guests in your home. Roya and Fahima can tell you that even our school is not safe for children back in Dand. Yasmine had the misfortune to step on a misplaced landmine at school. We are just so happy we did not lose her. We can deal with one less leg."

"I'm sure one less leg doesn't slow her down," says Basra. "With such a beautiful head of hair and face, no one will even notice." She cups her hand around Yasmine's chin and admires the deep, dark eyes that complete her youthful face.

"Oh, Basra, you must also meet our other two male chaperones," Omar comes around the truck with Pooch on a rope. "This is Hawa and Omar's youngest son, Omar, and his little brother, Pooch."

"Indeed, Fahima," Basra looks at Omar and then down at Pooch.

"Madame Basra, I hope it is alright to bring my little brother here. He really is very good in the house. If you do not like animals in the house he can stay in the truck, but he will cry."

Basra pets Pooch's head and then looks up at Omar, "Young man it would be unkind of me to make your little brother sleep in the truck. He is welcome inside, too."

"Basra," I laugh, "You are too kind. We invade your home like a horde of locusts, and you just smile and accommodate us. May Allah always smile kindly on you for your generosity."

"Well, Fahima, shall we go in and have some tea? I am sure these travelers are weary and thirsty. There is room in the courtyard in the shade for the children to move around and play. I'm sure the back of that truck is hard on them."

"Thank you, Madame Basra," Fawigia carries Laila while Hakim and Noor dash for the door and the courtyard. Monisa helps Yasmine maneuver the uneven street and into the cool of the house.

Shafika pulls at Sakina's sleeve as Sakina heads for the house door. "Mother, may we go to the market?"

"Shafika, we just got here. Oh, it has been a long ride and you and Nooria have been very good to help with the little ones. You will need a chaperone. If Ghulam will go, you may go."

Shafika looks askant at Ghulam. He says, "Shafika I have to attend to the truck and my leg is not well enough to stand on long. Maybe Omar will go with you?"

Shafika shifts her glance from Ghulam to Omar, who is standing waiting for Pooch to finish sniffing an old wrapper lying in the street.

"Please, Omar," Shafika pleads. Omar looks to Ghulam and then to Fahima.

"It's alright, Omar," I say. "Just keep the house in view and take Pooch with you."

"Yes, Fahima," Omar flashes an embarrassed, uncomfortable grin. He looks down at Pooch and says, "Come on, Pooch, let's guard the girls while they shop. That will be new for us." He runs his hand down Pooch's shaggy back and waits for Shafika to lead the way.

"Just an hour and then right back," instructs Sakina. "Stay together and stay with Omar and Pooch. Nooria, do you have money?"

"A little, Mother."

"Well, not too long and do not spend a lot. Remember, we are all in a truck. Not much room."

"Yes, Mother. Come on, Shafika, let's get your curiosity …" her words fade as Shafika darts ahead, with Omar and Yasmine following just behind.

"Slow down," barks Nooria. "Yasmine needs time to walk the street."

Shafika stops and waits for the group to catch up, but she is already in front of a booth selling hair accessories and head coverings.

"Look, Nooria, do you think Monisa will fix my hair with these barrettes?"

"First, you really need to wash it," quips Nooria with her commonsense tone.

"Monisa is really good," adds Yasmine. "She did my hair so my bald spot won't show until it grew back in enough to cover. She worked in Kabul as a hairdresser."

Omar and Pooch walk along on the street side and stand behind the girls as they look over the displays of goods. "Pooch, so this is what girls think about."

"Not always, Omar," quips Nooria. "But we do like to look nice."

"Of course," adds Yasmine. "How else do you think we can get the attention of boys?"

"I'm sure I don't know," replies Omar with a bit of sarcasm in his tone. "To be honest, I have no idea how girls think or understand what they do and why."

Shafika turns and looks at him, "Well, we can help you with that." She smiles and turns back to continue looking at the array of hair things. The woman behind the stand laughs and offers to show Shafika a tortoiseshell clip.

"This would look beautiful with your full hair," the vendor notes.

"Too old for you, Shafika," says Nooria in her practical way.

"Oh, Nooria, you are always such a damper on my fun."

"Someone has to be," Nooria says quietly under her breath.

After ten minutes of looking through the bins, the girls decide to move on.

"Wait," says Yasmine. "I need the restroom and I don't think I can make it back to Madame Basra's." She whispers this to Nooria so Omar will not hear.

"All right," says Nooria. "There must be a public one here. We do have to stay together. Omar, we girls need to make a detour. Please come with us, but not too closely."

"I don't understand." Omar steps back with a quizzical expression on his face. Nooria whispers the situation and what they plan to do, and he blushes red and just shakes his head to acknowledge he understands.

Nooria waits with Pooch and begins asking Omar questions about living on the farm. Yasmine walks close to the wall of the building on one side of the alley to help keep her balance. Minutes pass, but no Shafika. Suddenly Pooch turns from the girls and points up the alley with a bark. He pulls at the end of the rope. Nooria turns in panic.

"Something is wrong," she says with a gasp. She looks down at Pooch, who is pulling at the rope trying to get down the alley. She calls, "Shafika!" but there is no answer. All three dash to the restroom door. Nooria beats on it. "Shafika! Shafika! Are you all right? No games!"

Nooria bursts open the door only to find it empty. "Shafika is gone."

"Where is she?" Nooria is panicked. Pooch is sniffing the ground and wants to head further up the alley.

"Omar, do you think Pooch can smell Shafika?" Nooria pleads.

"I don't know, but he sure wants to head up this alley. Do you think she came out and went the wrong way?"

"I don't think so, she could easily see us at the end. Why would she head away from the market and us?"

"Let's follow Pooch," says Omar, fearful he let them down as chaperone.

"What else can we do?" says Nooria. "Yasmine, you stay here in case somehow we missed her."

"Yes, Nooria."

"Come on, Omar, let's let Pooch go." Pooch continues down the alley with his nose in the air and then on the ground. The alley turns, and in the middle lays one of Shafika's shoes. Pooch sniffs it and stops.

"Oh Allah, Omar. That's Shafika's shoe. Why would one of her shoes be here?"

"Nooria, we must get Ghulam and Fahima. Something serious has happened to Shafika. Pooch and I will stay here. Take Yasmine back and get them." The dread in Omar's voice sends a shiver through Nooria.

"You are right. Be careful. I'll take Yasmine back and get mother and Ghulam and Fahima."

"Hurry," says Omar.

Chapter 28:
ROYA—SEND IN THE WOMEN

Qandahar, Day 3

"Basra, how are your children and grandchildren?" I am anxious to understand how those in the villages larger than Dand are faring.

"Ah Roya, these are difficult times. There is little work for my grandsons, and my children are finding it difficult to provide for their families. The fighting continues to plague our lives, as I'm sure it does you in the smaller villages. We are always keeping an eye on our girls and sometimes even the boys."

"Kabul is the same, maybe worse," adds Monisa. "I was there for three years but had to leave finally."

"Oh yes," Basra pours more tea. "I have heard that the Taliban has stripped women of all privileges there and they must strictly follow Sharia Law."

"Is that not the case here in Quandahar, Basra?" I ask.

"It is, but there are less Taliban fighters here so enforcement is not so strict. Fahima, how is it in the villages?"

Mother pauses for a moment to gather her thoughts. "We have more freedom from the Taliban, but our own militia imposes restrictions on us 'for our own safety,' so they say."

"Really," Basra sets the teapot down and sits at the table between Monisa and me. "Is Kashar still leading your militia?"

"Yes," replies Mother. "Both Rahmat and Ghulam were taken to help in the fight. Fortunately, Kashar is using Rahmat as his accountant, so he is not required to carry a weapon and engage in the fighting. Ghulam, on the other hand, was a fighter then was wounded. He was sent home to heal, and that is why we have the luxury of him for our chaperone."

"Fahima, I am so sorry. Do you think the limp will go away?" Basra reaches across the table and puts her hand on Mother's.

"Only Allah knows, Basra."

At that moment, the street door bursts open and Nooria runs in. "Nooria why are you running?" I jump to my feet. Before I can say anything else, Sakina rushes to her.

"Nooria, what is the matter. This is not like you."

"Mother, we cannot find Shafika…"

"What?" Sakina embraces her.

"Nooria, tell us what happened," Mother says. Basra stands and calls for Hassan.

"We were looking at hair things when Yasmine needed the bathroom. We went together, Omar and Pooch and I stayed at the opening of the alley. Yasmine came back, but Shafika did not. Pooch barked and pulled to go up the alley and then …"

"What, darling, what?" Mother said.

"Then we found Shafika's shoe in the middle of the alley."

"Monisa!" I shout. "Come, we must find Shafika."

Monisa jumps up, "Roya, let's go. I need to get in the truck first, you go ahead. Ghulam, you go with Roya. Fahima, you, Basra, and Sakina stay here and send Hassan when he comes down."

Ghulam and I head up the street, Ghulam struggling to keep up with his injured leg. I see Yasmine at the opening of the alley. "Which way, Yasmine? Where are Omar and Pooch?"

"Omar followed Pooch up the alley and they went around the corner." Yasmine begins to cry.

"It will be alright, Yasmine," I hug her to help stop her shaking. "You go back to Basra's. We can look for Shafika."

"I'm sorry, Roya. I should have stayed with her."

"It's alright, Yasmine. You didn't do anything wrong. Please go back to the house so you are safe. Your mother will be anxious." She turns and heads down the street to Basra's door. Up the street comes Hassan, Basra's husband. He is old and rather slow. Ghulam and I decide to go on and not wait for him or Monisa.

"Ghulam, let me go on ahead, I'll be alright. It is so hard for you to stay up with me."

"Sorry, Roya. I feel less manly not being able to protect or help you."

"You are doing more than you know just by being here. When Monisa catches up, direct her to follow me. Once I find Omar and Pooch, we can split up if we have to."

"That's wise, Roya. Go on, we need to find her as quickly as possible. If someone has taken her, either they will take her away or harm her right here."

"I can't think of that right now, Ghulam. I have to focus on just finding her."

"Be careful, Roya, there are many disrespectful men here. You know what I mean."

"That's what I am afraid of, Ghulam. We have to find her fast."

We continue up the alley and I break into a run, leaving Ghulam behind. Around another corner I see Omar and Pooch. Pooch is jumping up on a door and barking. "Omar!" He turns and sees me running up the alley.

"Pooch thinks she is in there," he points to the heavy door.

As I catch up, I shout Shafika's name. There are screams coming from behind the door. It sounds like a chair being knocked over. Pooch continues to bark as Omar pounds on the door.

"Shafika, are you in there?" I shout at the top of my lungs. There is a muffled response, but we are not sure if it is Shafika or not. Omar tries to break the door with his shoulder. He is too small to budge it. Ghulam is coming, and behind him are Hassan and Monisa.

In the blink of an eye, Pooch jumps down from the door and jumps through a small window to the left of the door. When Omar and I look through the broken window, we see an older man holding his hand over Shafika's mouth and a knife at her throat.

The man is old but muscular and has a tight grip on Shafika.

"Get that dog out of here or I will kill her," shouts the abductor. He pulls the knife closer to Shafika's neck.

I plead with him. "Please, don't hurt her. What do you want?"

"I have what I want," he replies with a nasty grin.

Omar tries to call Pooch back through the window so he can get the rope on him, but Pooch will not relent. I can hear Monisa running up the alley and Hassan's footsteps behind her. I don't know what to say. I know that in a minute this man is going to leave with her, and he will hurt her if we try to intervene. Halfway through my thought process, Monisa catches up to us. She pushes Omar and I away from the window and uncovers something she has wrapped in a small scarf. She braces herself against the wall below the window and raises something that reflects the sunlight through the window.

"Is that girl worth your life?" she says in a slow, calm voice. She is pointing a Russian-made pistol at the man's forehead. "I am a very good shot. Trained by the Russians. Now drop the knife and let her go."

At first the man looked skeptical that she even knew how to use the gun. Ghulam came up at that moment behind Monisa. "I know how to use the gun," he said. "One way or another, you are not getting out of here with the girl."

Once the man saw Ghulam and the gun, he dropped the knife and ran out another door with Pooch on his trail. Shafika opened the door and I pulled her out into the alley and embraced her. She was so frightened she couldn't even cry for a few minutes. Once she realized she was safe, the tears poured down her face.

Omar chased Pooch. "Omar, be careful," I warned, then turned to Hassan who had finally made it down to where we were.

"Did someone have her?" Hassan asked, out of breath.

"Some older man," Monisa said. "He looked older, but still pretty strong. He had a knife to Shafika's throat."

"I know this old storage room. I suspect I know the man, too. He is not very honorable and has tried before to grab other girls. I'm surprised Basra did not warn them before they went to the market. That dog sure saved the day."

"Pooch and Monisa and her Russian fashion accessory," quipped Ghulam. Hassan looked down and saw the gun in Monisa's hand.

"Well, I haven't seen one of these in a long time. It's a Russian TT-33 Tokarev pistol. Thirty caliber, right?" Hassan takes the pistol from Monisa's hand and inspects it.

"I don't know the specifics of this thing," says Monisa, "but it's not the first time I have needed to persuade a gentlemen that he didn't want to do what he thought he did."

Ghulam laughs, "Monisa, Kashar could use you. You are fearless."

"Fearless or a little stupid, Ghulam. Not sure which."

Omar comes back with Pooch on the rope and says the man disappeared in the labyrinth of buildings connected to the alley.

"Well young people, you have handled this situation well. We'd better get back to the women and mothers and let them know all has ended well," Hassan puts an arm around Ghulam's shoulders and all head up the alley and back to Basra and Hassan's home.

Chapter 29:
FAHIMA—ANOTHER DANGER OVERCOME

Qandahar, Day 3

"Oh, Shafika darling, are you alright?" Sakina, Basra, and I meet the rescue party and the shaken girls at the door. Sakina rushes to Shafika and embraces her with tears in her eyes.

"Shafika, what happened," Sakina moves Shafika to arms' length and looks her up and down to check if she was physically harmed.

Shafika wipes tears from her eyes and rubs the red mark on her neck where the man was holding the knife. "I think I'm alright, Mother. I just can't stop shaking." Sakina embraces her again and mutters, "Thank you, Allah, thank you!" Shafika's shoulders are quaking despite her mother's tight hold.

"Fahima, I am so sorry. I forgot to warn the girls of the danger that lurks in our streets." Basra is frantically looking from one girl to the other.

"Oh Basra," I comfort, "Even though we are from a small village, the girls are aware of the dangers. Even out in country these things happen. Thank Allah we were able to get her back before any harm was done." I turn and look for Pooch and Monisa. "It seems we have two very good guardians in unexpected packages with Monisa and Pooch. Monisa, I hope you will allow Ghulam to help you manage your "gentleman persuader". Now that the children know we have a weapon, they will be curious about it. Given that we are all living in the back of a truck for a little while longer, proper precautions should be made."

"You're right, Fahima," Monisa hands the pistol, wrapped again in the scarf, to Ghulam. "Here, Ghulam. Lock this in the cab of the truck so the children cannot get to it."

Maky looks at Noor, who is intently interested in what's wrapped in the scarf. "Noor, that is not a toy and nothing you should be touching. Understood?"

"Yes, Mother," Noor turns his gaze away from Monisa, and looks up sincerely at his mother and nods his head.

"That goes for both of you, too, Hashim and Wakil," says Fawigia as she extends the warning to her sons. "Little men need to grow up before they may use guns. When you are big like Ghulam, you may know guns."

"Unfortunately, there is more truth in that than we can admit," says Hassan. "Men in our country seem determined to use guns to settle things. Allah is not smiling on us."

"Well, young people, how about a hot meal to turn your thoughts to other things?" offers Basra. "We would like your stay in Qandahar to be more pleasant than it has started out to be."

"Thank you, Basra. I'm sure these growing bodies are ready for some nourishment. I look to Roya, "Roya, you and Monisa please gather up the little ones and take them back to the courtyard. You big girls may sit out there, too, until our meal is ready. Basra, Sakina, Fawigia, and I will be happy to help you to prepare. Ghulam, please put the gun safely away. Omar, please take Pooch for a walk close to the house so he is ready to be indoors."

Each group notes their assignment and heads off silently.

"Tomorrow we will take the children for their vaccinations and call Ahmad and Mahmoud to let them know their families are here." I look to Sakina and Maky, "Ladies, let's not let the men know what happened today. It is difficult enough for them to be away and not able to protect their children and wives."

"You are wise, Fahima," says Hassan. "There can be too much sometimes on men's minds to bear."

"Come, ladies," says Basra. "Let's prepare these lovely guests of mine a hearty meal. To the kitchen."

Basra sets raw vegetables on the table and Sakina and Maky begin peeling them. Maky looks to Sakina and says, "Sakina I am so sorry to put your daughters in danger because of my son. If I hadn't asked Fahima to help me keep Noor out of the madrassa, we wouldn't be in this position."

Sakina places her hand on Maky's and says, "Maky, my girls have always been in danger. The death of my sister's husband was just the final straw."

"Yasmine's accident," interjects Fawigia as she draws water for rice, "Was my sign that I need to take my children to a safer place. Where in Afghanistan is a safer place, I still do not know, but I trust Fahima to help us get to that place."

"As mothers, we look out for and protect our children," I say. "Over the years I have endured the disrespect and lack of ability to lead a faithful and productive life because of the will of the zealot men who restrict our every hope and dream. Our journey is about freedom and safety for all of us—children, women, even our men. Our country struggles to move forward with the rest of the world. The zealots do not even want women to know of the rest of the world and what mankind is doing. Going backward to an age of fundamental laws like Sharia is holding us all back. I can only imagine what the rest of the world thinks of us."

"Fahima, do you really believe we can overcome everything working against us?" Fawigia speaks as she pours the water for rice in the pot, then sits down suddenly and begins to cry.

"Oh, Fawigia," I try to reassure her, "I do believe Allah is on our side. I know the devastation to your beautiful Yasmine makes you feel guilty and unable to protect all your children, but there is strength in our belief and hope in our future. This I know."

"Fahima, may Allah always bless you," said Sakina, "For being so wise and so generous to include all of us in your quest."

"Ah, Sakina, this is not my quest. This is for all of Afghanistan, if only one small venture into a better way of life."

Chapter 30:
KASHAR—SECRETS UNFOLD

Leaving Omar and Hawa's Farm

"Rahmat, I have been told that Ghulam and your wife and daughter were at Omar's farm just before we arrived. Is that true?" *If they were there, I don't understand why they left before seeing him. It has been months since the men have had a chance to go home.*

"Yes Kashar, Hawa mentioned that they were there to pick up some supplies. They are taking a few of the children to Qandahar for their vaccinations."

"Is this because your daughter is their teacher?" *That does seem strange to me. Why these children and not all the others?*

"According to Hawa, Ghulam is seeing a doctor for his wound and acting as chaperone for the group. The other women have no other male in their family to accompany them, so Hawa says."

"I see. Your wife does like to get in the middle of village business, does she not? Even when it does not concern her."

"Fahima finds being confined to the village with no work tedious. She does try to help where she can. Since Roya is the village schoolteacher, I suppose she is really helping Roya. I'm also sure she would want to supervise Ghulam's doctor's visit."

"Your wife is most attentive to your adult children, Rahmat. Are they not old enough to handle those matters on their own?" *This whole conversation annoys me. Fahima has played a major part in the disruption of my family, and the very thought of her running off to Qandahar with a group of mothers and their children seems to be more of her meddling.*

"To tell the truth Kashar, I think Fahima is always looking for a reason to get to the city. The Taliban restrictions and our inability to always have the militia in all villages to protect them gives them a very limited life. She knows the Taliban will allow travel for the week of vaccinations, and I believe she saw it as her opportunity to get away, briefly. She does have cousins in Qandahar she will probably visit as well."

"I see. So you believe she and Roya are with Ghulam and the others headed for Qandahar."

"Yes, if Hawa's information is accurate, and I have no reason to believe it is not."

"I do not trust the Talibs to peacefully allow the women and children to travel to Qandahar and back without incident. They always find a reason to chastise our women for some Sharia sin. We should go to Qandahar to ensure the vaccination week does not end in tragedy."

"I agree, Kashar." Rahmat seems genuine in his agreement, but he may just want the opportunity to see his family. The men have so little chance to go home.

"You probably think I am agreeing just to see my family, and you would be correct. You are fortunate to have your sons with you, and with the death of your wife you have no need to travel home to see her."

"Rahmat, you stupid lout. You might remember that it was your wife who encouraged my Maryan to go to Kabul and apply for university. The Taliban put a swift end to her dream and her with the acid they flung in her face for not dressing properly. By all that is holy, I still cannot forgive Fahima for filling my wife's head with thoughts of education and ultimately getting her killed by the Taliban."

"Kashar, I am sorry your beloved is gone and your sons are without a mother, unlike my son and daughter. But to make Fahima responsible for that is unfair. Fahima merely told Maryan of her experience in university when King Zahir was ruling. She did not suggest or encourage your Maryan to go do the same. I truly understand your anger, but the very forces we are fighting against are to blame for your wife's horrible death. To that end you and the rest of our militia continue to fight."

"Enough. I do not wish to dwell on this anymore. We will return these supplies to base camp and then go to Qandahar to see how the vaccination week is proceeding. And Rahmat, see that your wife has not encouraged any other women to do something to enrage the Taliban."

"I understand, Kashar."

Chapter 31:
FAHIMA—PEACE IN A MOSQUE

End of Vaccination Week in Qandahar

"Basra, after prayers today we will be leaving Qandahar. Ghulam and Omar, with the help of your Hassan, have readied the truck as much as is possible." Basra and I lay out our prayer rugs at the back of her mosque. It feels so peaceful to pray in a mosque again, amid other people. It is not safe to pray in our village mosque. Ours has become structurally unsound because of the bombing and gunfire between the Talibs and our militia. This one is much more elegant, and a little safer.

"Fahima, we have enjoyed having you and your mothers and their children. Travel does not happen often, and our grown children and grandchildren are in other parts of Afghanistan. Hassan and I are happy to share what we have with you and your extended family."

"Without your help, this mission would have been much harder, but now we must leave your comfortable home and travel on to find our destiny."

"Oh Fahima, I do fear for you. You are so brave to leave the relative safety of the village you were born in to seek a better place to prepare for your grown children and what someday might be your grandchildren."

"I cannot even begin to think of Ghulam and Roya married with children. They both despair for their own reasons. I miss Rahmat. It has been months since we have been together. Ghulam is only home because of his wounds. There are no young men in the village right now that Roya could marry. We exist in this unnatural world of women and old men. Even though Sakina's and Maky's husbands have avoided being conscripted into the militia or the Afghan army, they must work in Qandahar to make enough money to provide support for their growing families. Will Nooria, Shafika, Yasmine, and little Laila have to live the same unnatural life my Roya has?"

"The Taliban is committed to dragging our nation back to ancient ways and reestablishing the old, outdated laws in these modern times, Fahima."

"What will happen to Noor and Hakim and little Wakil and Jalil, still in Maky's arms? Will they be forced to the madrassa and indoctrinated into the mujahadeen? Will they become sacrificial lambs and blow themselves up in the name of Allah, or more accurately in the name of the zealot religious leaders who have forced this Jihad on us and the rest of Afghanistan and the outside world they believe are infidels?"

"Fahima, where have you gotten the inspiration and strength to attempt this escape? It seems to me that only Allah can persuade an educated and reasonable woman, as I have known you to be your whole life, to push your way past the men of our culture. Has Allah shown you a better world if you are willing to seek it?"

We are both kneeling on our prayer rugs at the back of the mosque, and I must laugh a little. The woman next to me hushes me, but I whisper to Basra, "I have seen a better life. For a moment, I was able to live it. I want that for my children and all the children of our country. I want the people of Afghanistan to benefit from the knowledge the world has accumulated to improve our lives and our minds. I am sick to death of marching in place. Moving backward. I want to join the world, not be hidden away to cook and clean and do nothing more. I want all the girls to learn to read and be educated and allowed to develop their own interests, to use all their Allah-given skills for the betterment of mankind and their families. I want the boys to have the same. Freedom. Education. Peace, Basra, peace. No more violence. No more bombs blowing off young girls' legs at school. Husbands and wives together raising their families."

Basra slowly shakes her head in acknowledgement, and we complete our prayers and begin the walk back to her home.

Chapter 32:
FAHIMA—LEG ONE TO BAMYAN

Outside Qandahar on the Road to Bamyan

"Omar, how do you like our adventure so far? Is Pooch content or does he want to be back at the farm?"

Over the roar of the motor of this aged truck he says, "We are both amazed at everything around us. I have never been this far from home, especially without any of my family members. Pooch, he loves the little boys playing with him and the attention the girls give him."

"Really Omar," says Ghulam as he tightens one hand around the steering wheel and shifts into another gear with the other. "Pooch likes the girls' attention, hey? How about you?" he winks at Omar and smiles at me.

I understand Ghulam's sly message. "Omar, I hope we haven't overwhelmed you with all these lovely girls all around you." Omar's face reddens. Ghulam and I chuckle together at his shyness.

"Just know, Omar, that I did promise your mother I would not bring you back with a wife. Is that alright with you?" His face gets even redder, but he does not say anything.

"Alright Ghulam let's not embarrass our co-pilot and mechanic more. We are grateful to have him along for all his skills."

Ghulam turns to look in the rearview mirror of the truck and changes his tone, "Mother, see that cloud of dust behind us?"

"Yes, Ghulam."

"That could be a patrol of Taliban fighters."

"Really. What should we do? We are only several miles out of Qandahar. Could they be looking for us?"

"I don't think so. Maybe we should innocently pull to the side of the road and let the children out for a few minutes until they pass. We could be returning home from vaccination week for all they know. The timing is still good."

"If they ask, where shall we say we are going?" *We should have had a story prepared before we left Qandahar,* I think.

"Mother, let's be sure all of the mothers have their heads properly covered and that they are not violating any of the Taliban's Sharia edicts."

"They won't bother the children, will they Ghulam?"

"Generally not, but the girls will have to act young and naïve. Have Nooria stay seated in the truck with Jalil on her lap so they believe she is already a mother. That should discourage any interest in her. She is the most mature of the girls."

"What about Roya and Monisa? Will they be interested in them?"

"It is hard to know, Mother. The more they act like mothers and married, the less interest the Talibs will have in them."

"Let's pull off quickly before they catch up to us so we can set the stage."

"Good idea. About 100 meters ahead there is a grove of trees. I will pull under it, and we can let everyone in back know what is going on. Oh, and Mother I will get the handgun out of the glove box just in case. I just want you to know I will have it out."

"Oh Ghulam, I pray to Allah that will not be needed. What will happen if they find it on you?"

"Clearly I am wounded and part of a militia. They will expect me to have a weapon. Hopefully they will just take it from me and send us on our way."

"Where shall I tell them we are going?"

"I think Ghazni is the best. It is big enough that if any of the Talib are from there it is possible they will not know of us."

"I just hope they don't ask us any questions about Ghazni. Our lie could unravel very quickly if we don't know anything about the city."

"We will have to chance it, Mother. Now hurry and get the ladies set up for our visitors. Omar, put Pooch on a rope and walk him, but keep him close. He is our second line of defense."

"I understand, Ghulam. I do have some cousins in Ghazni, so I will mention their names if it comes to that."

"Good boy."

I jump out of the passenger door and quickly head to the back of the truck. Monisa is already out and heading my way. "Monisa—"

"I see the cloud behind us, Fahima. I know what that means."

"Monisa, you and Roya have to look like mothers. You grab Hakim or Noor and Roya can grab Laila and look like they are your children. Stay seated in the back of the truck out of the light so they cannot see you well. We must protect Nooria. She can sit back here too, with Jalil. Have you ever been to Ghazni?"

"What? No."

"That will be our story. We are on our way home to Ghazni, so we have reason to be on this road heading in that direction. They might ask us specifics about Ghazni, but we will just have to do our best to convince them that is where we are from."

"Got it."

I step up into the truck to instruct the rest of the group. "Boys, you may get out and stretch your legs a bit. Stay close to Shafika and Yasmine. You can help Omar walk Pooch."

The three boys quickly jump out and head for Omar and Pooch, who are standing at the front of the truck.

"Sakina, Maky, and Fawigia just be your normal mothering selves. Maky, I want Nooria to hold Jalil, so she looks like a mother, and Fawigia I want Roya to hold Laila. They will both stay in the back of the truck with those little ones."

"Fahima, what is it?" Sakina asks.

"It looks like a patrol of Taliban might be coming up behind us. Our story is that we are on our way home from the vaccination in Qandahar. We are going home to Ghazni. Has anyone been to Ghazni or know anything about that city? They may question us, and I have never been there."

"My mother's uncle is the collector in Ghazni, Fahima," Fawigia says. "He might not be liked, so I will not use his name. I know a little about the town from things my mother has told me. I will try and do the best I can to remember but be vague."

"Good, Fawigia. We must all have our heads covered. Let us make sure nothing we are wearing is against Taliban laws. One little thing could ruin our charade. Monisa? Let us have a look." I scan her up and down. "I don't see anything objectionable."

"Great," she says with a heavy dose of sarcasm. She is my worry.

"Fahima, I'm scared," Maky clutches Jalil, then reluctantly hands him over to Nooria.

"Will he sit with Nooria, Maky?" I ask.

"He might cry and beg for me. On this trip he has hardly been out of my arms. He is rather spoiled."

Roya interjects, "Actually, if we have crying children the Taliban might go on their way quickly to get away from the upset."

"Clever girl, Roya. Alright, let us get in our positions. I can hear the trucks nearing." I help Maky and Sakina out and then help Fawigia lift Yasmine down. Yasmine adjusts her artificial leg and steps over with Shafika.

"Yasmine, be sure the men in the patrol see your artificial leg." I hate to make a point of her leg, but she is so beautiful that a man seeing that leg might be discouraged and not pay her any attention.

Ghulam rounds the back of the truck. "Inshallah Mother, they are almost here. Does everyone know what to do?"

"I hope so. Please round Hakim up so Monisa has a child."

"Yes," Ghulam acknowledges my request and heads back to where the little boys are.

"Everyone ready? This will not be our first test, but it could be our most dangerous."

Chapter 33:
OMAR—BOY SOLDIERS

Stopped on the Road to Bamyan

"Come on, Pooch," I give the rope a pull to get the dog away from whatever it is he is sniffing and head him back to the truck. It looks like Ghulam has gotten everyone back under the cover of the truck. I need to hurry back and get ready for the patrol, should they decide to stop and check us.

"Omar," Ghulam limps around to the front of the truck. "You need to help in this deception. They might think I am militia, so I am going to pretend to be very wounded and asleep. You need to act like you are in charge of this party. Can you do that?"

"I will do my best."

"Good, I'm getting into the truck on the passenger side and pretend to be unconscious. You will need to do all the talking. Can you do that?"

"I have talked to enough of Walizada's drug guys to know what not to say. I will try to act like I'm in charge and say what they expect me to say."

"I know you can do this, Omar. You are a very smart young man."

I help Ghulam up into the passenger side of the truck and look back to see how far the patrol is behind us. "Come on, Pooch. You stay with me." The shaggy beast looks up at me and pushes his head against my hand for a pet. "Okay, okay. Please be on your best behavior. This is serious business. Ghulam, they are about half a kilometer away."

"Get ready, Omar. Don't say any more than you must. Stay respectful. Inshallah."

After a few minutes, three small pickup trucks pull in behind the truck. Each truck bed has six or seven Taliban fighters with weapons in them. All stop in a line, and a short young man who is heavily armed gets out and walks toward me.

"Inshallah. Who are you and where are you going?" he asks in a clipped voice.

"I am Omar. I am escorting these women and children home from Qandahar where the children were vaccinated." I start to say more than stop. He ignores me and looks through the truck window at Ghulam slumped in the front seat.

"Who is he?" The young man adjusts the rifle over his shoulder, then brings it down and pokes the barrel through the driver's side window.

"He is my idiot cousin. He does not speak. He was stupid enough to step on an IED. He went to Qandahar with us to see the doctor." I look the Talib in the eye to see if he believes me and then divert my look like I would with the farm animals, so I appear submissive.

"Ah, he looks stupid. He is lucky he did not hurt anything more than his leg. We make our IEDs to kill, you know." He grins and pulls the barrel down, then turns his attention to the back of the truck.

"Well, let's see what you have back here." He walks to the back of the truck, pulling the barrel of his rifle up again. I tighten my hold on Pooch. Pooch might think he is going to hurt the girls and boys and attack him. I have no doubt this guy would shoot poor Pooch on the spot. As he walks to the back, three more Talib jump out of the first truck and begin to walk up.

"Fine looking cargo you have here," says the first man once he gets to the back of the truck and looks in. "Fine indeed. Lots of nice females."

"And their children," I quickly note.

"They can't all be married, I think. That one with the flowered skirt?"

"She is my sister. Poor girl lost part of her leg. Do you see?" Yasmine hears what I say to him and moves her artificial limb so he can clearly see it.

"Too bad. She would make a tasty wife."

At that moment, Jalil decides he no longer wants to sit on Nooria's lap and starts crying and holding his little arms out to his mother. Maky and Nooria try to calm him, but he is not contented. Maky tries to ignore him, but he persists.

"Ah," says the man clearly annoyed by the racket the toddler is putting up. "Babies, who needs them?"

"We all started as babies," I say and then wish I hadn't. It sounds to demeaning to him. At that moment, the other three walk up and he is distracted. The man moves away from the back of the truck and over to the new group. He speaks to them quietly and then turns back to me.

"So, Omar," he says in a mocking way. "Which one of these females is yours?" he turns back to look at each one in the truck.

"These are cousins and of course my sister. My woman is at home. She is pregnant and did not want to come with us. I am helping these family women out by driving them to the vaccination." He looks me up and down like he doesn't believe I have a pregnant wife. I'm not sure I believe it either, but it makes for a logical story. I hope he believes me.

"Well, by my count you have six women, two girls, and four children. This is going to cost you."

"What do you mean, cost me?"

"There are tariffs on this road. The Taliban owns everything. You must pay."

"I am only the driver," I offer. "The women will have to come up with the money for you."

"Well, tell them they owe 500 in transport fees." He then walks back to the group. I am sure Fahima heard our conversation and knows what we owe. I go to the back again. As I am moving back, I look closer at the three new Talib who have joined the first. They are boys, hardly bigger than Noor. They have at least two ammunition belts across their chests each and a rifle that is almost as tall as they are. They can barely walk upright with the weight of their weapons. These are the boy soldiers Walizada and his men talk about. They are right out of the madrassa. I cannot see Noor like this, but that is what would happen if Fahima had not taken on this journey.

Fahima hands me the money they demand. I walk back to the group, but the boy soldiers have noticed Pooch and are petting him. Pooch seems to sense that these boys are not dangerous, and he licks and jumps for them. They delight in his antics, just like Noor and the other little boys would. Now I understand why my parents kept me on the farm—so I would not have to go to the madrassas and become a fighter for the Jihad. I have been allowed to grow up and be a kid. These boys will never know that. They may not even live to be grown up. How sad. How tragic.

I hand the money to the first man. He turns to his soldiers playing with Pooch and yells at them to get back in the truck. He turns to me and says, "Thank you, pilgrim. And thank your ladies for me too." He pretends to doff a hat and bows mockingly, then turns and heads to his truck. Within a minute, they have all pulled away and headed up the road.

I hurry to the back of the truck to let the ladies know they have gone and then to Ghulam.

"Excellent job, Omar," Ghulam climbs out of the truck and pats my back. "You are pretty good at thinking on your feet." At that moment, Fahima walks up.

"You certainly did handle them well, Omar. Your mother would be enormously proud of you."

"Fahima, did you see how young those boy soldiers were? I have heard about them but had no idea they were younger than me."

Fahima smiles, "Now you better understand why we are going to Bamyan and need to save Noor and Hakim from the madrassa. Mullah Aman was ready to take Noor."

"I used to think my mother and father were overly protective of me and I would like to go to the madrassa, but now I see the result. Little boys playing soldier and dying for the benefit of other men. When they cannot convince men to join them, they use boys. I cannot believe Allah agrees with that.

"Well," Fahima says, "Nor do I."

"Come, Mother," Ghulam says. "We need to give them some time to get ahead of us and then continue on our way to Bamyan."

"You are right, Ghulam. Let us let everyone out of the truck for a quick break, then we must continue on." She bends down to Pooch, "And thank you, sir, for understanding how to treat our enemies and entertaining them while we negotiate our way down the road." She pats him on the head and turns to go to the back of the truck and help everyone out.

Chapter 34:
ROYA—ENEMIES ABOUND

Back on the Road to Bamyan

"Roya," whispers Monisa as the truck rattles down the road again to Bamyan. "Have you ever met Kashar?"

"No. Why do you ask?"

"It is well known that he is not a fan of your mother. I just wondered if you had ever seen or talked to him. Or he to you. Just wondered what the head of a local militia was like and why he dislikes your mother so much."

I adjust Laila on my lap, then reply, "Mother and father do not speak of it. From what I gather, Kashar's wife, Maryan, was inspired by Mother to attend university even though she already had two small sons. When she went to Kabul to apply for admittance, she was approached by the Morality Police for wearing something inappropriate—white shoes, I think the story goes."

"Yes, I know that rule. Everyone in Kabul knows that rule," Monisa remarks.

"Well, Maryan was from a small village and not aware of the restriction. Anyway, an older Talib, it is said, took it upon himself to punish her and threw acid in her face."

"You see many women in Kabul with scarred and uglied faces from that punishment."

"Well, Maryan suffered for several days and died before Kashar could get to her. I think he can't forgive himself for not keeping her from going, but more importantly he blames Mother for giving her the notion to try to get her education."

"He had two sons?"

"Yes, Zalmai and Ahmad. Kashar raised them with the help of his mother, and now those two are about the same age as Ghulam and I and are active members of their father's militia. I hear they are very brave fighters. Ghulam says they are devoutly loyal to their father."

"Well, if Kashar raised them you can imagine how important he is to them."

"You can also imagine how much of Kashar's hatred of Mother they have absorbed. Ghulam says he had to completely avoid them in camp. Kashar keeps Father around to do all the bookkeeping for the militia and repairs on the equipment since he is the most educated and trustworthy. Strange that Kashar would trust Father so much when he hates Mother. He needs Father but takes his pent-up animosity out on Ghulam. I would not be surprised if Ghulam's injury was friendly fire, as they say."

"I have heard that term from Sergio. Fighting men seem to have their own way of punishing one another." Monisa grabs the bench as the truck rumbles over another hole in the road. She slides back to sit on the rough wood of the seat and adds, "It must be extremely hard for all of them. Young men without a mother. Father and sons victimized by the mere example of their wife and mother. Men—they can be their own worst enemies."

"True," I say, then add, "Women can do the same. Hate can be like a cancer—a malignant growth that pushes out the healthy thoughts and love."

"It seems easy to see the difference and for people to want to shed the hate and resentment for the joy and peace of harmony, but something in our nature just won't let us let it go," Monisa says.

"I have read that the Buddhists understand life in a different way. They worship the peace of forgiving and the joy of nonviolence. I hope we find that in Bamyan. We can find similar teachings in our Qur'an, but our faith has wandered off that path. If the Buddhists can accept us after all the Taliban has done to destroy their sacred monuments, then there is a lesson for we Muslims."

"A lesson, yes," Monisa notes sadly, "But to get the Afghan culture to embrace it or even to acknowledge what is written in our own sacred writings is an impossible task. We have been reading and interpreting our own faith's writings for eons and still here we are."

"Stuck, regrettably in our original sin. May Allah forgive us."

Chapter 35:
FAHIMA—DRUG LORD'S HOSTAGE

Continuing on the Road to Bamyan

"Ghulam, do you have any idea how much further to Bamyan?" After the encounter with the Taliban patrol, I am growing more and more weary of the many dangers we are exposed to here on the road.

"I'm not sure, Mother. I have never traveled this way before. With the militia, we stayed in our own territory south of Qandahar. Going north as we are to Bamyan, I cannot judge."

"I understand, Dear. How do you think this old truck is faring?"

"Better than expected. Between Omar and Allah, it is holding together and will hopefully get us to Bamyan."

"Without this truck we are totally vulnerable out here," I say, thinking out loud.

Ghulam laughs, "Even with a tank we would be vulnerable out here on the road. Besides the Talib there are bandits, drug lords, other militias, the UN, and American troops. All manner of combatants are roaming around."

"Thanks for that cheery thought, Son." I wince at his words and quickly say a brief prayer to Allah asking Him yet again to help us along. "How is our fuel level?"

"I'm not sure I can rely on this gauge, but it looks like we have consumed about three-quarters of a tank. We can go maybe another thirty kilometers and then we will need more. What do you think, Omar?"

Omar stirs from a quick nap and says, "I think these old trucks do not have reliable fuel gauges, so knowing how much petrol is left is mostly luck in my experience."

"I would agree," says Ghulam as he taps on the gauge to make sure it is set correctly. "Bumping around on these rough roads and the amount of dirt and debris the truck takes on affects the little things quicker than the main mechanical pieces."

"Do you think it will be easy to find more petrol along here? I did not anticipate that being a problem. In fact, the thought of enough fuel never entered my mind."

"I know, Mother. That is something Father would have tended to. We will just have to keep an eye out and get some wherever we can. Omar, do you know how to siphon petrol out of another vehicle's tank? We may have to resort to checking these disabled vehicles along the road if we do not find a proper petrol station."

"Ghulam, one of the first lessons you learn on the farm is siphoning petrol from one vehicle or piece of equipment to another. It's an unpleasant job my brothers always gave to me. I'm actually pretty good at it. Let us hope there is a length of hose in this truck somewhere to be able to do it. I am guessing most old trucks like this have a hose stored somewhere just for that purpose."

"You're right. The militia trucks we use always have a hose because we are always looking for more petrol."

"Well, I am going to let you two gentlemen handle the petrol problem. It seems you have a better idea of what to do than I." I will still worry, but at least I have them thinking ahead. My Ghulam is so like his father—practical, quick, smart. Omar is also clever and practical. I would expect nothing less from one of Hawa's boys.

I closed my eyes for what seems like just a moment and awaken to a late afternoon sun. "Ghulam, where are we?"

"We have traveled about forty kilometers and are now in need of petrol. Omar and I have been scouring the roadsides looking for a station or something we can borrow from. There was a sign about half a kilometer back indicating a petrol station ahead. We are really hoping the sign is current and the station does exist and has petrol to purchase."

"Is it likely?"

"It's pretty deserted on this stretch of road, but I am hoping the sign is correct."

"We should know in a few minutes," says Omar, spotting a station on the left side of the road. "It looks like a station coming up on the left."

"You're right, Omar," Ghulam leans against the steering wheel and cleans the windshield to see better. "It's just coming into view. Mother, let's hope Allah is smiling on us and we can purchase some here."

I see it coming into my view. There seems to be a cluster of small pickup trucks parked around it. "Ghulam, what do you make of the trucks parked around it?"

"I don't know, Mother, but I would say it is not a good sign. Unfortunately, we cannot pass this up. We may not find another before we run out."

"Can you tell if it is more Talib?"

"The Talib patrols usually have more men. I only see a few. Maybe it will just be travelers like us."

"Inshallah. Inshallah."

Ghulam pulls the truck in beside a large petrol tank and turns the engine off. It shudders and shakes before cutting out. I quickly get out to let the passengers in the back know we are stopping for fuel. They need a break from riding around in the back like that. I'm sure the children will need to relieve themselves and stretch their little legs. The fresh air and sun will do them good.

As I'm helping the mothers get out of the back, Ghulam and Omar go in to see if there is any fuel to purchase. Maky hands me Jahil and climbs out ahead of Monisa and Sakina. Yasmine is the last to get down, with the help of Nooria. As we all walk up to the building to get out of the sun, we hear conversation. Ghulam is talking to three men inside. I cannot hear exactly what they are saying, but they are all laughing. That seems safe. Then suddenly I hear a scuffle and Omar is pushed out the front of the small station door. I do not understand.

"So, this is the poppy-grower's son," mocks a large man in dirty clothes with a large knife in his belt and a handgun pointed at Omar.

Ghulam appears in the doorframe and is pushed outside by another roughly dressed man. "Azizi, look, we also have one of Kashar's men. This is our lucky day."

Monisa comes up next to me and whispers, "I think these are some of Walizada's men. That's why they recognize Omar."

Ghulam speaks, "Hey, we are here escorting these women and children. We do not wish any harm."

The first man holding Omar by the arm says, "You don't wish us any harm, huh?" He laughs. "And what harm could you possibly do to us? You are a man with a limp and a battle wound I would say and this young boy. What, are the women going to attack us?" The other man pushing Ghulam out the door laughs and spits on the road.

"Look what we have here," says Azizi to his comrade. "One of Kashar's men, a precious son of Omar our poppy grower, and a whole bunch of females."

"With children," Ghulam adds, but they both laugh the comment off.

"Hey, Azizi, don't you think Walizada would like all these bargaining chips? Good leverage."

"Ghayous, you are right. Walizada might even reward us for bringing him all these pilgrims." They both laugh again as they push Ghulam and Omar together and Azizi comes around behind our cluster of women.

"One problem," says Ghayous. "They won't all fit in our truck, and that old truck won't make it back to our camp."

"I guess we will have to pick the most valuable," grins Azizi. "What do you think, Ghayous?"

During this confrontation, Monisa has quietly sneaked back to the passenger side of the truck where she is not seen. *I know she is looking for that pistol. Please, Allah, do not let this come to a deadly end.*

"Azizi, I think the women and children are too much trouble and Walizada really has no use for them. The young girls, now, that is another thing."

Sakina grabs Nooria and Shafika and pushes them behind her. Roya stands in front of Yasmine.

"So, Ghayous, which has the highest value to Walizada and therefore us?"

"If the militia man were one of Kashar's sons, he would have value, but he is not. I would say that the poppy grower's son has the most value. Old man Omar would be totally in our control if he thought his son's life was at risk." They both laugh and spit together.

"It's agreed then. We will take the drug grower's son as hostage. I'm sure Walizada will be pleased with our gift."

Azizi roughly grabs Omar's shoulders and pushes him toward their truck. The men in the other trucks stay inside the station and do not offer any help. They must be travelers like us and know the ruthlessness of the drug gangs. These two men are certainly part of the Walizada drug cartel and will do whatever it takes to get their way. Ghayous pulls a gun from his belt, points it at Omar, and waves him toward their truck. At that moment we hear a growl, and Pooch launches forward and tries to grab the hand with the gun. Ghayous takes that gun hand and hits Pooch in the head with the gun, sending him to the ground. He is stunned for a moment.

"Don't shoot him," screams Omar.

Ghayous laughs and draws the end of the gun down on Pooch's head.

"Ghayous," says Azizi, "don't waste ammunition on a damn dog. Let's get this kid in the truck and take off before those men inside decide to be brave."

Ghayous pulls the revolver back and continues to walk to the truck.

I keep thinking Monisa is going to appear with her gun, and this is going to end with shooting, but she does not. The two men put Omar in the truck between them and drive off. I help Ghulam up and look to the men inside, now standing outside the door watching the truck drive off with their hostage. None make eye contact with me and quickly get in their vehicles and drive off. We are left there alone in a whirl of dust with the station manager. I have no idea what we do next. Finally, the station manager speaks, "Woman, what are you doing out here on the road with all these children?" He stares at me and rubs his graying beard.

"Sir, we have come from the vaccinations at Qandahar."

"I see. And where are you headed?"

"We are bound for Bamyan." I hesitate to tell the truth but cannot imagine this old man could do any more harm to us then those we have already encountered.

"Who was that young man the drug lords just drove off with?"

"He is the son of one of their poppy growers. He is the youngest of a friend of mine."

"Well, I hope his father has the right stuff to get him back in one piece. The drug cartels are not merciful unless you have something they want. I am surprised they did not take your young girls. Besides the drugs, that is what they value most."

"Praise Allah," I reply to him. "Omar is precious too, but the girls would have fared far worse with those two than Omar will."

"You are right, Lady. Now, can I help you with some petrol?"

"Do you have some to sell?" asks Ghulam, dusting himself off. "We are going to need a full tank to get where we are going. Sir, would you have a mobile? We need to call Omar's father and my father about what happened. We cannot get Omar back by ourselves."

The old man looks Ghulam up and down, and then assesses the circle of women and says, "Yes, you are certainly going to need help. I do have a mobile inside for emergencies. Please come in, and we will see that you can make those calls. Ladies, please come in out of the sun and rest. I have some sweets for the children. May Allah bless them."

"Thank you," I say resignedly. "May Allah bless you, sir, for your kindness."

Chapter 36:
KASHAR—EXTRANEOUS RESCUE

Militia Encampment, South of Qandahar

Kashar, Rahmat, and three fighters pull into the north encampment after their trip to Omar and Hawa's. The three fighters unload the truck while Kashar and Rahmat go to Kashar's tent.

"Rahmat, make sure the inventory of the new supplies we have just secured is properly updated. Things seem to disappear when they think we are not keeping track."

"As always, Kashar."

Rahmat seems distracted. He does not know that I am aware his wife, son, and others have fled Dand and are headed out of Qandahar. His conversation with Hawa was overheard.

"Also, Rahmat …"

"Yes?" He looks up, still lost in his own thoughts and with a worried wrinkle in his brow.

"Rahmat, I know Fahima, Roya, and Ghulam are fleeing Dand from their trip to Qandahar. Do you know where they are going?"

"Hawa would not tell me, but I suspect Fahima did not tell her to keep her safe. Fahima does have Omar and Hawa's youngest son with them, Omar. I understand, Kashar, if you are angry. My wife has withstood all the violence and isolation she can. Where she believes she will find respite from all that, I am not even aware."

"You know she makes our position more dangerous by spreading out the territory and people we are committed to protect."

"I do understand. I am here. She and I have not spoken in months. She will usually listen to me, and I can reason with her. On her own, she is a fighter in her own way."

"She is more grief to me than you know, Rahmat. Now she brings on more. She is insufferable. She is a danger to herself and all those she can convince to follow her. Now she has headed out into the Taliban and drug-lord world where it is even harder to protect her and the others."

"I know her intentions were good, Kashar. That is why I love her so."

"Foolish man married to a foolish woman. What else is to be said?"

At that moment, Zalmai, Kashar's oldest son, enters the tent. "Father, I have an urgent call from Ghulam."

In unison Rahmat and Kashar say, "Ghulam?!"

"Yes. He is calling from a petrol station south of Ghazni."

"Ghazni? Well, Rahmat now I guess we can imagine she is heading for Hazara country."

"My guess, Kashar, is she is headed for Bamyan."

"Father, Ghulam reports that when they stopped for fuel two of Walizada's men were there."

"Let me guess, Son. They took the young girls."

"No, Father. Actually, they have taken young Omar as a hostage back to Walizada."

"Well, at least they were smart enough to grab a bargaining chip and have not taken the females for their own pleasure. Zalmai, send a truck of men to Omar's farm and wait for me there."

"Yes, Father," Zalmai turns and heads out of the tent into the encampment.

"Well Rahmat, it didn't take your Fahima long to get herself in trouble. Now we must forget what we were doing and run to the aid of Omar and Hawa. Damn, I hate that woman of yours. This is going to cost me some weapons. Walizada is always looking for more weapons."

Rahmat remains silent and only nods his head.

"I want you to stay here, Rahmat, in case there are other calls from her. I am going to negotiate with Walizada to get the boy back. Then we will talk about your wife's escape to Hazara country."

"Yes, Kashar." Rahmat watches as Kashar exits the tent and begins shouting orders to men to load weapons in the transport truck. Rahmat lifts his head and says a silent prayer to Allah to keep everyone safe. He smiles slightly to himself, thinking about the boldness of his sweet Fahima to undertake such a dangerous journey.

Chapter 37:
FAHIMA—MOVING ON

On the Road North of Ghazni

"Mother, are you all right?" Ghulam shakes me from my thoughts and silent prayers.

"Yes, Son. I am just praying to Allah that He will keep Omar safe, and I must admit I am also praying that Kashar will get involved and retrieve Omar from Walizada and return him safely to his parents. I am also praying that Hawa will not be too angry with me for letting her baby be taken by those drug lords so they can manipulate Omar, and Kashar for that matter. I wish they had taken me."

"Hawa knew this was a dangerous mission. She knew she was putting Omar in danger but believed enough in you to do it."

"Yes, Ghulam, but I have failed, and we are very early on in this adventure. There will be many more challenges. Of that, I am sure."

"We have to leave much in the hands of both Allah and Kashar. I know from fighting with Kashar that he will not let Walizada terrorize Omar and his family. Walizada does need Omar and his sons to grow the poppies. Kashar needs to keep Walizada under some control. Kashar does have the power to bring Walizada in line. Walizada has more money, but Kashar has more men and weapons. And Walizada has an illegal business at stake. If Kashar wanted to, he could shut down Walizada."

"This all seems so far from Allah's plan for us. Drugs, guns, money, men fighting men. None of it seems wise or practical, and that's coming from a woman like me."

"Few women see things the way you do, Mother. Many men, including Kashar, believe women are inferior in common sense and practical reasoning. Father and I know that is not the case with you."

"Thank you, Son, but being able to see through all this mess just makes life harder for me. I know there is a better way."

"Soon, Mother, you will have your chance to try your theories out. Bamyan lies just ahead."

"Praise Allah, we have gotten here without any more pain. Thank you, Ghulam, for being such an important part of this." I turn and hug him as he pulls to the side of the road.

"Where do we go now, Mother? To the refugee camp?"

"No Ghulam. We may end up there, but we do have some money to give everyone a decent night's sleep and bath in a hotel. We will refresh and then figure out where we will go and what we will do next. This is a high point where we can get a view of the whole valley. Look, in the distance you can see one of the caverns where the Buddha statues were. From here, Bamyan looks like a peaceful valley in the bosom of the mountains. I hope it will prove to be our peace-filled valley."

"It does look like a place Allah smiled on," Ghulam says. "Let us get the others out and let them have a look. We all need a perspective on what could happen next."

We walk to the back of the truck and help everyone out. Noor has Pooch by the rope. Without Omar here, Pooch is relying on Noor as his guide.

"Fahima," Fawigia is holding Laila and lending a sturdy arm to Yasmine as she maneuvers over the uneven ground. "Fahima, do I need to call my relatives in Hazara for a place to stay tonight? Where will we find a mobile?"

"Don't worry, Fawigia, we will figure all that out tomorrow. Tonight, we will stay in a hotel, and sleep in a real bed and take warm-water baths. Once we are clean and fully rested, we will begin to figure out our next steps."

"Fahima, Mahmoud left me all the money he had," says Sakina. "I can help pay for our stay."

"That is very generous Sakina but hold on to your money. We are going to need it to provide for ourselves. Our money is the only difference between us and the people in the refugee camp." I turn to Nooria, Shafika, and Yasmine. "So, young ladies, what do you think so far?"

Shafika is the first to answer. "It looks so green. The mountains surrounding the city look safe, like we are in the arms of Allah."

"Girls, it may look peaceful, but we must still be on alert," Roya, always the teacher, reminds them that Bamyan is a city, not the small village they are used to and that things can happen to young girls.

"This place is nothing like Kabul," says Monisa. "It seems quiet. Orderly. After my years in Kabul, I could use a little quiet and order."

"I almost didn't believe we could get here, Fahima," says Maky, with tears in her eyes. "I have felt so guilty that my need to keep Noor out of the madrassa pushed all of us out of our small village. But now that we are here, I am glad we had the spark of Noor to get us to move. This place does seem peaceful and hopeful. Peaceful and hopeful. I did not want to completely believe a place like this existed. Thank you, Fahima, for having such a vision."

"Oh, my dear, I didn't know for sure either. But let us remember we have a long way to go to fit in here and reestablish our lives. I fear the worst is not over yet."

"There is still much to overcome, you are right, Mother," says Roya. "But we have accomplished a lot so far. Let us not forget that. Just getting here is an accomplishment. And we did overcome some challenges along the way."

"You are right, darling," I answer. "I do wish Omar were here to enjoy it with us. Tomorrow we will have to ensure Kashar is going to correct that situation and get Omar back from being a hostage of Walizada and his men. We must not lose that focus."

"Omar is now a part of our family of refugees, and we will keep him in our hearts and minds, Aunt Fahima," Nooria says, with such conviction for a young one.

"Of course, we will. Now, let us take a quick break before we get down into our new city and find some hotel rooms."

Chapter 38:
RAHMAT—SONS TO SAVE

Kashar's Encampment

"Zalmai, have you heard from your father yet?" I pray to Allah that Kashar is able to get Walizada to accept the weapons he is offering to return young Omar to his family. My Fahima will never rest until all the children are safe, especially Hawa and Omar's youngest. Hawa understood the risks when she allowed Omar to accompany them, but Fahima will never forgive herself if anything happens to him. "Any word, from Kashar?"

"No, Rahmat. Father has not sent any sign that the negotiations are complete and Omar back with his family," Zalmai looks at his mobile again to see if he has missed a call or if one was dropped. "We can only wait here as instructed until Father returns or sends word."

"Maybe we should pray for everyone's safe return?" I know Zalmai is not interested in trusting in Allah and believes his father can accomplish all things, but Kashar may need divine intervention in this operation.

"Don't be ridiculous, Rahmat. Father will deal with Walizada and get Omar back. This is what he does. This is why he is head of the militia and not you." Zalmai turns his back on me and walks to the table where Kashar has maps and stacks of paper, running his fingers across the edge of the table, almost in tribute.

"So, I will pray for all of us."

"Pray for that crazy wife of yours. Her foolish actions have put Omar in danger. As always, Father must correct the failures of others. He is the one who must deal with the evil and threats to our people."

"I understand your point of view, Zalmai. But Fahima was trying to save the women and children from our village, just in a different, nonviolent way from your father's. Her intentions are as good as are your father's."

"How can she believe a woman can lead such an operation? We are here to protect the women and children. Right?"

"I know you were raised without your mother and, so far, have only a small idea of what women can do, but let me tell you that women are much more capable than you may imagine. Of course, they do not have the strength to fight as your father does, but they are smart and brave, and Fahima is as smart and brave as any. And, may I add, sincerely intent on helping others."

"Putting others in danger with foolish notions, don't you mean?"

"I think we can all agree that the violence that has smothered our village life and stolen the ability to sleep calmly in our beds at night without fear is not her fault. Men wage war. The Taliban has pushed women into overly protected corners of their lives and stripped them of the ability to do anything but tend their households and worship. Fahima knows there is more to life than that, and she has grown intolerant of living in fear and restriction."

"Fear and restriction, hah? She is willful and foolish."

"Maybe, but not for herself, for others. Much like your mother." At the mention of his mother, Zalmai swings around and steps within inches of me.

"Don't mention my mother. I didn't even know her."

"And why didn't you know her? Because the violence of our culture and the teachings of the Taliban destroyed her. The very violence that Fahima is trying to escape is what took her from you."

"Silence!"

"Zalmai, Fahima and I knew your mother. She, too, was trying to escape the fear and repression by getting more education. She was thwarted by the same violent men that we combat today. Don't you think that part of what drives your father is revenge for what happened to your mother and his protection of the women and children that are left – including you and your brother, Ahmad?"

"There is no question that my father is still angry over the loss of my mother."

"Your father's anger fuels his actions. At some point, we must stop all this contention and violence and get back to the business of obeying Allah and raising our families to be fruitful and peaceful. That is a rare way of life in Afghanistan. It seems we are always at war here, but there are places in the world where people live and worship without violence and bullying zealots. Your mother was looking for that way of life."

"Rahmat, you are a foolish old man. Without your ability to keep books and engineer things, you would be as useless as your crazy wife." Zalmai looks at me with the same expression his father uses. *Because I choose not to fight with weapons, they believe I am only half a man. They do not understand that I already know where all this violence is leading, and I do not want to contribute to it. I was forced to join the militia, but have found a way to be useful without carrying a gun.*

At that moment, Zalmai glances at the mobile vibrating in his hand. "It's a call from Father." He slides a finger across the screen and puts the phone to his ear. After listening for a few moments, he shuts it off and turns to me.

"Father needs cash, Rahmat. Walizada wants money and weapons to release Omar to his family."

"I see. How much does he need?"

"He said 2500 more."

"Come. Take me to the weapons depot. I have money reserved there that we can take for the hostage release."

"Let's hurry. Father said Walizada is growing impatient."

"Zalmai, we must be careful. This could be a trick of Walizada to find out where our weapons cache is stored. There could be someone watching us. Walizada is that greedy and clever."

"Let's go, Rahmat." Zalmai finds a set of keys on Kashar's table and heads out.

"How many men shall we take?" I ask.

"He instructed that it should be just you and me. The fewer that know where the weapons are stored, the better."

"So, we will have no protection if we are being followed?"

"Come on, Rahmat. I will take care of us. You just get the money. Father is waiting."

I have no choice but to follow Zalmai to the truck. We are both silent as we drive the five kilometers outside camp into the mountains to get the required money. Two miles out of camp, we notice a vehicle following us about half a kilometer behind.

"You were right, Rahmat. This is a Walizada trick to find out where we are storing our weapons. I will have to lead them away and lose those who follow us before we can go and get the money."

Zalmai goes off road and heads for a bend and a place to hide so the truck behind thinks they have lost us. "There are clusters of trees around this bend, they will think we have gone into one of them. Once they are past us, we can circle back." Zalmai slides the truck behind a tall stand of reeds along a creek bed and turns the engine off. We sit silently for several minutes, listening for the motor of the other truck. Finally, it rushes past and, after a minute's wait, Zalmai starts the engine and we backtrack to our turning-off point.

Within ten minutes we are at the cache. I have kept watch to ensure the other truck has not picked up our trail again.

"Go, Rahmat. Get the cash and let's get out of here."

I rush in, and behind a large boulder is a carved crevice where a money bag is stored. I pull it out, count out what is required, and head back to Zalmai who is waiting at the truck. I am about five meters from the truck when I hear the other truck approach. Zalmai has pulled his handgun and is crouched behind the driver's side door of the truck. Before I realize what is happening, I hear gunfire and feel a hot jolt to my chest. I start for a moment and fall to my knees. I can smell something with a metallic bite and realize it is the blood coming through my shirt. I fall forward and black out.

Chapter 39:
ROYA—NEW ALLY

Bamyan Hotel

"Come, Yasmine, let me help you down the stairs. We will meet everyone at the breakfast table." I offer Yasmine my left arm as we slowly manage the stairs to the hotel lobby and the serving area. She refuses it and balances herself with the handrail.

"Mistress Roya, I have never been in a hotel before. This is very wonderful."

"Don't get too used to it, darling, we cannot afford to spend what little money we have on such luxuries going forward, but my mother thought it important for us to rest properly, clean up, and eat before we set out to re-establish our lives here."

"I'm excited to do that. This seems like a wonderful place to live."

"Well, we all hope it will be better than Dand, but there are no guarantees. We will all have to work together to make it home. There are still dangers even here in Bamyan, remember?"

"Yes, ma'am. I will remember."

"Good. Let's join the others." Once at the bottom of the stairs we make our way through a narrow hall, which opens into the lobby and the small serving area to the left. Sitting at multiple tables are Mother, Ghulam, and the other mothers and children.

"Any word about Omar, Ghulam?"

He looks down then replies, "No, nothing yet."

"Come, Roya," says Mother. "Have some breakfast, then we can go to the mosque for prayers. We all need to ask Allah to bring Omar safely home to his parents. We need to pray that Kashar can successful negotiate with Walizada to return him."

"Ghulam," Mother turns to him. "Why don't you take Noor and Hakim out with you to check on Pooch. See how he is doing in the truck and bring him the scraps from our breakfast."

"Of course, Mother." Ghulam finishes his tea and gathers the little boys to go to the truck.

"Oh, Ghulam, please check with the desk and see if Kashar has called and left a message."

"Yes, Mother, I shall."

"Come, Roya, there is some tea left." Mother turns back to us and gives her seat at the table to Yasmine. "Monisa, would you stay here with the children while we go to the mosque to pray?"

"Yes, Cousin Fahima. I can do that. Praying is not really my thing, as you know." Monisa flashes her a grin and begins to round up Laila and Wakil, then takes Jahlil from Maky. "Come with me, little man," she coos to Jahil. "We are going to check out our new town. Come kiddoes, Aunt Monisa will take you on a tour."

"Can you handle all of them, Monisa?" Fawigia asks.

"Sure. I have Nooria, Shafika, and Yasmine to help. We will be fine. Please, go to mosque and pray for us all."

"Mother, I will stay behind and have some breakfast."

"Alright, Roya. We will be back in an hour or so. Come, ladies. It is time for prayers," Mother says, then she and the others leave and

Monisa heads out the back door with her army of children. I relish the alone time and the quiet. I'm used to living with Mother and Grandmother Uzra, these days with all the children and other mothers has been noisy, chaotic, and a little overwhelming.

As I sip my tea and enjoy the buttered croissant I found on the table, a young woman approaches. She looks about my age. Her head is covered, and she is wearing pants and a blouse. The vest she wears over the top has many pockets. She looks like a fashion model posed as an archaeologist. All she is missing is the pith hat.

"Good morning," says the young woman as she walks up to my table. "Are you alone? May I join you?"

"I am alone now," I say with a smile, "but if you had arrived five minutes sooner you would have encountered the crowd I am with."

"I see. Well, it must be nice to have so many people around you. I am alone right now."

"I am Roya." I extend my hand. She gives me a warm handshake and sits down across the table from me.

"Hi. I am Sarah." She waves for a server and orders tea and toast. "I'm guessing you and your party arrived last night since I have not seen you before."

"We did. We are here from Qandahar. We had taken the children there for vaccinations."

"Is Bamyan home for all of you?"

"No," I say, "but we are hoping to settle here. It's a long, complicated story why and how we got here.

"I would guess so," she says and looks me over, as I do her.

"You are not in traditional dress," I feel safe to note.

"No, I am not an Afghani. Actually, I am Lebanese. I am here with UNESCO to inventory the heritage sites. I am a forensic archeologist."

"How exciting," I can only imagine how different from my life her life must be.

"And you?" asks Sarah the forensic archaeologist.

"I am a teacher in my small village. As you probably know, here in Afghanistan women have been restricted from higher education, or any education at all, and are not allowed to work outside of the home. I am lucky to be allowed to teach and to teach girls to read. Even allowing girls to learn to read is not allowed by the Taliban."

"I have heard. I cannot imagine. It must be awfully hard for you. You seem educated." She reaches across the table and gently places her hand on mine.

"Even harder, because my mother and father are both educated."

"Ah, they are old enough to have been of that age when King Zahir was ruling. Loving all old things, I have studied the history of Afghanistan and know the story. In Lebanon, we have certainly had our wars and religious rebellions, but the plight of women has not been pushed back as severely as it has here. Is that why you left your village?"

"My poor mother couldn't take the violence and the restrictions anymore. The trigger was when the Mullah was coming for one of my brightest students, an eight-year-old boy destined for the madrassa. Funny that it was the plight of a little boy that pushed Mother to do something."

"She must be very brave. And smart," Sarah noted and sipped her tea while waiting for me to reply.

"Oh, she is."

"Well, I hope I can meet her soon. So, you as a group picked up, went to Qandahar, and are now arriving here to start over? Is that what I am getting from your comments?"

"That's our story. We know no one here but believed since the Taliban had already been through here and destroyed the Buddhas that they would not be back."

"And that is pretty well true," agrees Sarah. "I have been here for more than a year and it has been pretty peaceful. There are NATO troops posted here to insure no further harm of the relics. Bamyan was designated a UNESCO World Heritage site. That's who I work for."

"It must be such interesting work," I gush with obvious envy.

"Well, if you like digging in the dirt and inventorying hunks of rock, I suppose so." She smiles. "But I am a history maniac, so I love it. Touching history is a real rush for me." She looks at me to see the expression on my face.

"It's not exactly what would send me into a rush, but I do envy your obvious higher education and freedom to see the world. You are a long way from Lebanon." We laugh together as she pours me more tea.

"I have to say, Roya, that you are the most interesting person I have run into so far in Bamyan. I am certainly eager to meet that mother of yours and the other ladies."

"I would say they will all be most interested in meeting you, too." We both pause to sip our tea and Sarah nibbles on her now cooled toast. "There are three adolescent girls who are students of mine. You will be a real-life example of why we came to Bamyan."

Chapter 40:
KASHAR—HOSTAGE PLAN GOES AWRY

Omar and Hawa's Farm

"Zalmai, where are you and Rahmat with the cash? Walizada is getting impatient," the mobile signal keeps fading in and out. I turn my back to Walizada as he rolls a cigarette impatiently and keeps trying to read my face to determine what is to happen. I finally get a stronger signal and hear Zalmai say, "Father, we ran into trouble."

"What kind of trouble, Son? Was it as I expected? The request for more cash was a move on Walizada's part to follow you to our stowaway place and steal all of our cash and weapons?"

"Yes, Father. Four men attacked Rahmat and I at the stash site. I have killed them all, but Rahmat was hit in the chest and is in bad shape. I am taking him to Qandahar for medical attention. I hope we make it. What are you going to do about Walizada now, without the extra cash he requested?"

"Dealing with him is never straightforward. He is always changing the deal in the middle. Right now, he holds the leverage with Omar's life. But he does not know you killed all his henchmen, and he still does not know where our storage site is located. He thinks he will be relieving me of all our cash and weapons. I will have to resolve this standoff quickly before word gets to him. Zalmai, take care of Rahmat and let us hope he can survive his wound. Much of our operation's details are in his head."

"I understand, Father. I am traveling as fast as I can to get him to a doctor. I do understand his value to us."

"Good, Son. Be careful and thank you for dispatching those men of Walizada's. You have kept us in the game for now. I will talk to you soon. Keep me updated on Rahmat's condition."

"I shall, Father."

I pause a moment before I turn back to Walizada. He must not read on my face what has happened. I need a moment to think through a new plan.

"Hawa, could we ask you for some tea?" She says nothing, but nods and heads to the house. "Walizada, while we wait for Zalmai and your money, shall we let Hawa prepare some tea?"

"Kashar, really? Tea now? Have you no whiskey?" Walizada laughs. He looks to the truck where Omar is sitting between two of his men. A smug smile spreads across his face, thinking he has the upper hand on me. And in truth, he does.

"It will take Zalmai an hour or so to get here with your money. We might as well keep Hawa busy so she will not do something foolish to get her son back. Come, surely a cup of tea will not jeopardize our dealings here. I am as anxious as you to complete things, but the extra cash you have requested will take time to get here."

"Hawa is a good cook," says Walizada. "Maybe we will get some real cooking as part of this deal. Ah, maybe I should have included that in our negotiations." He laughs again and looks toward the house, where Hawa has already headed. He knows he has the leverage, and is enjoying the position he is in.

"Let's go in and see what she can fix for us."

Walizada and I head for the door, and the cluster of men we both have brought with us move behind us and stop at the kitchen door where they all light cigarettes to wait.

Omar and his three other sons are nowhere to be seen. I hope they are not planning anything foolish to rescue young Omar. I would suspect Walizada has men posted with them to discourage their interference and has kept them out of my sight and that of my men. There is more than just young Omar's life at stake here. Omar's whole family could be in danger if things go badly. Walizada is unpredictable and has a hair trigger when frustrated. My men are at risk also.

As we walk through the back door Hawa says, "Come, gentlemen. Please sit at my table and I will prepare a hot breakfast for you. I was in the process of that for my family when you arrived, so it is almost ready. Please, sit." She indicates two chairs at the table. Two teacups are placed there, already brimming with hot tea. I take the chair directly facing the back door. This position gives me a view of the men outside and any approaching vehicle. Walizada takes the chair next to me so he also has a view of the door and yard, but not as direct a view as I. He is no fool.

"Ah, Hawa your husband speaks highly of your cooking," Walizada says as he cools his tea with a hearty swipe of his hand across the top of the cup. "All your sons look healthy and well fed."

"Thank you, Walizada." Hawa keeps her back to him at the sink. She does not want to let him see the disdain in her eyes. She is straining to be civil. Her family's lives are at stake.

"Hawa, are Omar and your sons in the fields this early in the morning?" I ask to distract Walizada and to determine where they are.

"Yes, they left for the barn just before you and Walizada arrived. There is always work to do."

"And I so appreciate their work," smirks Walizada. "They help make my business the success it is."

Hawa does not reply. Nor I. *I still cannot determine where they are. Omar knew Walizada was bringing his son home today and relying on me to negotiate to get him back. Maybe he thought it would be easier for me to deal with Walizada if he and his other sons were not here. Maybe he thought Walizada would have less leverage if he and his sons were not here to become hostages too.*

Walizada needs Omar and his sons for the precious poppies. He is not likely to risk them, but he could take Hawa and young Omar. What will he do if he realizes he is not getting my cache of weapons and cash as he thought he would? Right now, I have more firepower with me than he does, but he has more men.

Hawa brings plates of warm food and sets them in front of us. We eat in silence. She pours more tea and clears the dirty plates away. Walizada and I stand and, as Walizada turns his back on us and begins to walk to the back door, Hawa walks up to him and sticks a large kitchen knife against his side, then signals for me to take the length of rope she has in her other hand and tie his hands.

She grabs the back of his coat and quietly says in his ear, "How dare you take my son? Did you think I would not fight for him?"

Walizada laughs. "What are you going to do Hawa, kill me? My men will kill your whole family and burn this place to the ground if you kill me."

"Maybe," says Hawa. "But Kashar's men are also here. It could be a fight to the finish, and you would be outmanned. I want my son back, unharmed. If I must kill you to do that, I will. I wring the necks of chickens all the time!"

At that moment, Omar and his sons come down from an upstairs room. They were not out in the fields. They did have a plan. Each is armed with a hunting shotgun. After I tie Walizada's hands, I take the knife from Hawa and point my handgun at Walizada.

"Walizada, are you going to die over a small young man? Hawa is right, my men can overpower yours. This is not the day for you to die. Tell your men to let young Omar go and leave. You may take the weapons I have brought in trade for your trouble. Tell them now!"

"Kashar, this is not over," Walizada hisses. I push him to the door, the barrel of my gun stuck in his back. First, he tells his men to get Omar out of the truck and let him come in. Then he tells them to load the weapons I have brought into their trucks. They think the deal is done and they have achieved their goal. Finally, I untie Walizada's hands and push him through the door. He walks past my men and to his waiting truck.

Young Omar runs in and is embraced by his mother and surrounded by his father and brothers. I envy such a strong family. Now I need to tell Hawa about Rahmat.

"Omar and Hawa, Walizada asked for more money to return Omar. His plan was to have us reveal where our weapons and money were cached so he could take that, too. Zalmai and Rahmat were ambushed going to get the money, and Rahmat was shot in the chest. Zalmai managed to kill four of Walizada's men. Zalmai has taken Rahmat to Qandahar. There was more to this exchange of Omar then you were aware."

"Praise Allah that Walizada is greedy, and his greed played against him," said Omar as he balanced on his crutch and hugged his youngest son. "And thank Allah for a brave and fearless wife." He looks over at Hawa.

"No question, Omar," I say, "Your wife is a tough one. You all helped save your young one. Walizada will be back, but he does need your poppies so he will play the game."

"Kashar," asks young Omar. "Do Fahima and Ghulam know Rahmat has been shot?"

"No, that is my next obligation. I must see to Rahmat. If you will excuse me, I must go to Qandahar. Omar, please be careful in the coming days. Walizada will not take this lying down. He has lost four men and not gotten the weapons and cash he was scheming for. I will leave some men here to help protect you. Although with Hawa on duty you may not need my protection."

They all laugh.

"Thank you, Kashar. May Allah bless you and your family." Hawa gives me a bear hug and I leave immediately for Qandahar.

Chapter 41:
NOOR—REUNION

One Year Later, in Bamyan

"Noor, please leave that dog alone and come in and get cleaned up," Mother says. "Your father will be here soon!"

"Pooch," I whisper into his shaggy ear, "Today is the day. Father is joining us in our new home at Bamyan. I have so much to tell him about our new life. Baba will not believe I have grown two full inches. I'm getting as tall as Ghulam. Ghulam says I have done a good job taking care of my mother and little brother. I hope Baba agrees. I hope Mother will tell him all the good things I have done."

"Let me scratch your other ear, Boy. I know you like that. Remember when we first came here? We lived in that big tent. Remember how you slept with me to keep me warm? I know, boy, you really missed Omar. We were so scared he would die when the bad drug guys took him. Thank goodness Kashar and his mother got him back. He's coming too, Pooch. Soon you will get to see him. I know you miss him, but I hope you will still be my dog too."

"I am anxious to show Baba how wonderful it is to live here. You and I, Pooch, can run everywhere and not be afraid of landmines. There are no Taliban fighters. The NATO soldiers are very kind. They don't shoot their guns like the Talib or Kashar's militia, but they do let me just look at them. Mother says they keep the peace. It's quiet here."

"Mother is so happy here. She laughs and smiles more. She goes out in public without her hijab. For some reason, she thinks that's a big deal. Ah, ladies! Right, Pooch?"

"Pooch, I really like living in such a big house with Hakim and Wakil and all the girls. The girls are a pain and try to boss me around, but it's like having a whole big family. We have good things to eat with all the ladies—Aunt Fahima, Aunt Roya, Aunt Monisa, Aunt Sakina, and Aunt Fawigia—taking turns doing the cooking. Mother was an alright cook, but between the aunties we have lots of good things."

"Pooch, I must introduce Baba to all of my new friends. There are older boys here. There are big boys here, too, like Omar and Ghulam. Soon I will be like them and have my father living with us. Baba has been working away from us since I was a baby. Here in Bamyan, he will live with us again. Mother is so happy about that. Me too, Pooch."

"Monisa promises me that we are going to sled down the big mountain here when winter comes again. Last year we did not have the proper clothes to enjoy the snow and that beautiful mountain. This year is different. That will be great fun, won't it, Pooch?"

"Pooch, we have to show Omar the mountain and how everyone skies and slides down it. He can borrow some of my winter clothes to come with us, right?"

"I must also tell Father that I am learning about Buddhism. I think he probably does not know about the Buddha and his teachings. Of course, I will have to show him our mosque where Mother and the aunties pray. Our new Imam is very nice. He is younger than Imam Ahmad, he likes to laugh and smile more. Everyone here seems to laugh and smile more. That's probably the best thing, right Pooch?"

"Well, come on we must get ready. Everyone is coming today!"

SHAFIKA—REUNION

One Year Later, in Bamyan

"Nooria, do you think Monisa will have time to fix my hair before Grandma Uzra, Father, and the others get here for the reunion?"

"Shafika, stop being so vain. You can fix your own hair. Monisa is busy," Nooria snaps.

"I know I can do it myself, but I want to look extra special for Father and Grandmother. We haven't seen them in a year. Besides, Omar is coming too."

"Yes, yes. They are all coming and we all must look are best." Nooria finishes folding the table linens she has just ironed and places them on the shelf.

"Sister, do you think they will like our new home?"

"Of course they will, silly. It is so much nicer here than in Dand. Mother and Father will be together again. We have this big old house, and we are all living here with Aunt Fahima and Cousin Roya and Ghulam. This is a happy place for us."

"Nooria, do you remember all we went through to get here? Remember the day Zahida died? The day Yasmine stepped on the IED and lost part of her leg? Those were really bad times."

"Yes, they were Shafika. That's why we have moved here," Nooria absentmindedly remarks as she continues her chores.

"We must introduce Father to Sarah. Sarah will be here, won't she?"

"Yes, Shafika, Sarah will be here for the party."

"I can't remember the last time we had a party in Dand."

"Those were sad times, Shafika. Not much to celebrate. Now we have much to thank Allah for and find joy in. We have a safe home. Mother is happy working in the community. Father will be joining us, and we will be a whole family again. Living with aunts and cousins is great, but having our father here with us and being the family Allah set us out to be will be the best."

"Oh, Nooria you are right. Being a whole family again is the best."

ROYA—REUNION

One Year Later, Bamyan

"Mother, where do you want me to put this tray of fruit?" She has been so worried, and everything must be in order for this reunion.

"Put it in a cool spot in the kitchen. Make sure the little boys and that dog can't get to it. Maybe up high." She continues dusting and sweeping our courtyard, readying things for the party.

"I know this is a silly question, Mother, but are you excited to see Father?"

"Roya, I am excited, but worried about the state we will find him in. The gunshot he took to the chest did a lot of damage. Thank Allah it did not kill him, but he could be so wounded he will not be the father and husband he used to be. Sometimes physical damage like that can inadvertently damage the spirit as well."

"But Mother, he should be elated to be coming to us finally, leaving Qandahar and Uncle Mahmoud's care to return to us."

"I am afraid it will not be as joyous as we could imagine. It has been some years since we were all together. His life and ours have walked different paths. I pray he is the kind, thoughtful, funny Rahmat I married, but life could have worn some of that away."

"I think you worry too much, Mother. I can't imagine that Father will be that changed. If nothing else, being reunited with you and I and

Ghulam may revive and turn the clock back for him. Look what it has done for us."

"You might be right, Roya. Coming here to Bamyan and the life we have begun to find has turned the clock back for me. I am working again. We can be an active part of the community. A community that is inclusive and safer. It really is like going to university again. New people with new ideas. Interesting conversations. Cultural events. Books." She almost giggles.

"Mother, thank you for taking the risks and the initiative to get us out of Dand and to a better place. Not just for us. Look at all the lives you have touched. The reunion today is bringing together the scattered family members of a variety of family trees. What started as a cluster of women trying to protect their children has mushroomed into a multi-gender event and the beginning of our own subcommunity here."

"I hadn't thought of it that way, Roya. Today's arrival of the fragments of our families to join us is quite extraordinary. Praise Allah He keeps them safe on their journey here. It will be wonderful to see Mother Uzra, Mahmoud, Maky's Ahmad, Hawa, and Omar."

"And of course Father."

"Yes, especially Rahmat."

"Mother, what do you think Kashar will think of our little venture?"

"Ah Kashar. It will be most interesting to see him again and hear what he thinks of our bold move. I understand he is bringing Zalmai and Ahmad with him as well."

"Do you think they will stay?"

"He has invested so much of himself in the militia and protecting our region that I think it will be hard for him to accept any other way of life. The violence has a way of pounding back reason and leaving behind nothing but raw instinct. Kashar might be to that point. I hope for his sake not, but I have seen it before."

"Do you think his sons are beyond the point of changing, too?"

"I cannot tell. I see the changes in Ghulam. Praise Allah his injury brought him back to us before he was too hardened. The real test will be your father. The years of violence and his wound may have done more psychological damage then we can repair."

"Mother, I know Father will find himself again with our care and love and Allah's blessings. He is a good man and will continue to be that."

"Yes, my darling, he was a very good man. I have prayed every day that Allah will return him to us with the ability to put the past behind him and live in the future with us."

"Mother, the future is where we all need to be heading."

"Yes, Roya, yes."

SARAH—REUNION

One Year Later, Bamyan

"Good morning, John. I have already ordered breakfast. May I pour you some tea while you wait for your order?"

"Good morning, Sarah. Tea would be fine." John seems to have slept well and is in a good mood. I am always nervous when the foundation board members come to see my work.

"Sarah, I have been reviewing your reports, and you have made excellent progress on the project. You are to be commended."

"Thank you. Allowing me extra help has really made a difference in our ability to process materials. Fahima has been a Godsent."

"She seems very bright and has picked up the details of foraging for relics well."

"Yes, John, she has. She is truly a remarkable lady."

"And you say her story is that she gathered up a group of the women in her small village and traveled here to find more freedom?"

"She did. And in the year she and her ladies have been here, they have done a textbook job of reinventing themselves. They went from small village domination by religious zealots, to a self-governing, self-supportive unit. It is quite amazing."

"Really." His order comes and he begins to eat. "Tell me more."

"To go back, Fahima was university educated as an economist back when the regime allowed women to be educated and work. She worked for the government in Kabul and then the Taliban took control and forced all women back to their homes. No work. No education."

"I am old enough to remember those times. It took our organization and the world a while to recognize what the Taliban was doing to the rights and dignity of Afghan women."

"Even in her small, isolated village, fighting and violence and living in fear dominated their lives. Finally, when a twelve-year-old girl was sold to a militia soldier by her mother and returned to the village violated and dead, Fahima had enough."

"We see this in a variety of cultures, unfortunately," says John as he sips tea. "Our organization is getting ready to launch a new project to help retrieve young women that have been caught up in the sex-trafficking trade."

"The irony of Fahima's story is that an eight-year-old boy is the spark that moved them to action. One of her neighbor's sons was being groomed by the local Imam to go to the madrassa."

"Ah, we have looked into those madrassas. An interesting cultural phenomenon. A school the conservative Muslims set up to pour stilted religious doctrine into young boys and brainwash them to fight in the Jihad. Their mothers readily send them because they believe they are getting an education. Reminds me of Hitler's youth programs."

"I guess every nationalistic group has their vehicle to recruit," I say.

"Cleverly, Fahima used the week of vaccinations to move the group without much notice out of their village and on the road here. She believed that since the Taliban had already come through here and destroyed the Buddhists' artifacts, it would be the safest place to start anew."

"Smart lady," John notes.

"So, they made it here and have been reinventing themselves and their lives ever since. Today is a big day. They have been here a year and the rest of their family members are joining them. I find it interesting that to these women it was very important to join whole families together. In their village, they were isolated from their men. Some had to work away, others were serving in the militia. It was a village of women, children, and old men. Today, not only are the women that were left behind coming, but the group is reuniting with their men."

"They are a sociologist's project waiting to happen, aren't they?" John smiles up at me. "Reuniting family units that have been segregated can be difficult. These women have been making their decisions and have become self-sufficient. Making room again for male figures could be tricky."

"More than tricky, John. Some of the marriages may fail. But at least the women are now able to carry on. If they had stayed in their village, they would have been destitute."

"Yes. Some Muslim cultures have yet to recognize parity in marriage and the need to support a family even after divorce."

"We have much work to do in the world, don't we John?"

"We do, Sarah. But seeing women fend for themselves and build the kind of life they believe is best for them and their children gives us hope, a small light shining in the darkness. Fahima has broken the tether."